TORMENTED

HEARTS IN THE

DARK

This book is a work of fiction. Any resemblance to actual events or persons, living or dead, is entirely coincidental.

"Tormented Hearts in the Dark," by J.J. Sweed. ISBN 978-1-63868-182-3.

For Jadon Sweed
and Leslie Sierra

TABLE OF CONTENTS:

THE HEAD AT THE CORNER OF THE ROOM

DUSK. PSYCHOLOGIST ALLISON CARMICHAEL never saw her patients this late in the day, but twenty-four year old Jermaine Braxton insisted on seeing him as soon as possible, ready to be placed under hypnosis. For the past week and a half, he's been having vivid dreams where he is unable to move, along with feeling a slight tremble on the side of his temple. As if someone had lit a firework in his brain, getting ready to explode. His bloodshot eyes have deep bags underneath them. Hollow, not being able to sleep well ever since he started to see the head at the corner of his room.

A head and nothing else. No body, just an oval-sized head with a long protruding nose that resembles something that of a witch. The veins hang down its neck like unexposed black wires. Bald as a full moon. And some nights, Jermaine can see its sharp crooked teeth. The eyes are wide enough that only the whites can be made out in the darkness. Jermaine can not look Doctor Carmichael in her own eyes. Thinking she would just be the head he could see and nothing else.

Jermaine shivers. The room was being kept cold by an overhanging fan that was nearly on full blast. It had been a hot September so far. Only to get ready for a blissfully cold winter in the city of New York. Doctor Carmichael's office, which also happened to be an apartment suite on the twelfth floor, could still hear the restless traffic that lingered down below. Cars honking at slow traffic, wishing they could just be home and not on the road behind some jerk-off. Yet Jermaine wasn't focused on the traffic down below, but the steady pace of the fan that swung above them. The soft clatter of the chain string bouncing off the light globes that shinned on the two down below. The last bit of sunlight casted small beams in between the shades that were partly closed. Large beads of sweat start to pour from Jermaine's face.

"Let's go over this one more time," Doctor Carmichael says, removing her glasses from her face to look directly at her patient with bright blue eyes, who had been lying down staring at the corner of her ceiling. "These dreams you've been having,"

"Nightmares," Jermaine says with a shudder.

"Nightmares, can you tell me what you're doing right before you fall asleep."

Jermaine lets out a sigh and shuts his eyes, "It's like I'm not even in my own body. You know, kind of like that out-of-body experience you hear sometimes on movies or TV. I can just see myself walking up to my lamp and turning it on. I haven't been able to fall asleep without it these past few weeks now. And I just lay down."

"You don't drink anything before falling asleep?" Doctor Carmichael asks while jotting down in her notebook.

"No," Jermaine said, listening more intently to the chain string hitting the globe above him. And was it by chance hitting it harder and faster now? "No, I don't drink anything before I go to bed. Not even a glass of water. And before you ask doc, no I don't smoke either. I don't take any kind of drugs that weren't prescribed by you."

Doctor Carmichael continued to write down in her notebook.

"Please," Jermaine opened his eyes. He turned his head over to Doctor Carmichael. Trying to contain the tears that kept his eyes red and wet. "Please can we just get this over with? I'm so tired. I just want to sleep in peace again without being tormented by…"

"By the floating head?" Allison Carmichael said. She said this with much sympathy.

The young black man wipes his forehead. His lip trembles as he nods his head.

Clearly, he's suffering from a horrible case of schizophrenia. Doctor Carmichael thinks to herself. *There is so much fear in his eyes that he believes it to be true.*

Doctor Carmichael pressed her lips together, nodding her head. Reaching over the side of her chair, she brings out a briefcase. Jermaine watches with slight enthusiasm. Doctor Carmichael opens up the briefcase. She takes out a wind-up timer, a dark indigo candle, matches, and a small vial of liquid that almost looks like honey. Under the table that sat between Jermaine and the doctor, she took a bag of small paper cups. She takes the cup, gets up from her seat, and goes to the corner of her office to her water dispenser. At this point, Jermaine looks away from the doctor. Not wanting to see if there would be a head without a body watching him with much delight. Smiling its wicked smile, as it has all those nights. He began to hear whispers all around him, making his skin crawl with goosebumps.

There is no help, the voices cried out to Jermaine. *There is no help, I am all you need. Let me out. Don't fight or I will bite, bite, BITE!*

Doctor Carmichael comes back with a cup of water and sets it on the table. She holds up the vial.

"This is an extract from a flower. It is only found in small parts of India. They call it Angel's Honey. It has a special

3

property that helps the patient dive deep into their subconscious to unblock anything that is deemed to be unstable for the host. It helps you relax. It'll also help with the hypnosis as I ask you questions to find out why you are experiencing these phenomena lately. Do you have any questions?"

Jermaine looks at the small vial with hope. Then a sudden wave of depression washed over him.

"It won't make me sick, will it? Like I won't hallucinate or go crazy?"

"Not at all," Carmichael says, taking the cap off the vial and dispersing the liquid into the cup of water, "I have done this plenty of times with my other patients. All of them, a total of seven patients, all responded well to the hypnosis. They are living out the best of their lives the last time I've heard. It will only make you feel tired. It'll be like falling asleep, while staying slightly conscious."

Jermaine watches as the doctor stirs the liquid in the cup. He swallows, hearing a click in his throat. Feeling more thirsty than he has ever been before. More sweat continues to pop out from his forehead. Looking up, he sees the fan still turning at the same speed. The *clink, clink, clink* of the chain string hitting the globe seemed to have grown quieter now.

"Do I have your consent to proceed with the hypnosis?" Doctor Carmichael asked, looking up at Jermaine, still stirring the cup.

"What?" Jermaine looks back down, his red eyes grown wide.

"Your consent. I need to know that what we're doing is what you want to continue with."

Jermaine licked his lips and nodded.

"Okay. Drink all of this down. Once you're finished I will turn the timer for a minute. Your eyes need to be closed. Just lay down and get comfy." Doctor Carmichael hands Jermaine the cup.

Jermaine looks into the cup. The liquid inside looked thick and smelled like a Mr. Clean product. Doctor Carmichael struck a match before lighting the candle. The sound of the match moving across the box made Jermaine jump. Nearly spilling the drink onto the floor. Now the fragrance grew stronger in the office. A fresh scent of lavender and what seemed to be vanilla wafted into Jermaine's nostrils. Jermaine took a small sip. To his surprise, the drink had absolutely no flavor to it. Despite its unusual smell, it was like sipping on air. He tipped the cup back. Swallowing the entire drink in two large gulps. His head already started to feel heavy and swimmy. Jermaine sets the cup back down, lays back on the couch and closes his eyes.

Doctor Carmichael wounds the timer back a minute and holds it. "Take three huge breaths in through your nose," she explains, "and out your mouth."

Jermaine does exactly what the doctor ordered. He began to notice the clinking sound from the chain above start to slow down a bit.

Clink (bite)... *Clink* (bite)... *Clink* (BITE)

Doctor Carmichael releases the knob on the timer as it begins to tick away.

"Can you still hear me, Jermaine?" Her voice now seemed far away, distant. And also very low.

Jermaine nods.

"I want you to go back to the very first day you saw this floating head. I want you to tell me what your room looks like. What you feel, what you hear. Can you do that for me?"

Jermaine nods again a little bit slower now.

"Good," Doctor Carmichael's voice is at a low bass. "When you hear the sound of the timer's chime, you will be in your room. You will tell me why this floating head sends you into a deep torment. When I say the words Angel's Honey you will come out of your hypnosis state and will be healed. Are you ready?"

Jermaine doesn't move. It almost looks like he's stopped breathing as well. Doctor Carmichael cocks her head to the side to examine him a bit closer. When she was about to ask again if he was ready Jermaine spoke in a low whisper.

"Yes."

Doctor Carmichael's eyes grew wide and her head popped back up, drawing closer to Jermaine. She had never heard anyone speak before the timer went off.

The timer chimed.

Jermaine takes a deep breath. Held it. Then relaxes. He was in a complete nirvana state. His eyes rolled around behind his eyelids.

"Jermaine," Doctor Carmichael said softly, "I want you to describe everything you're seeing until you see the floating head."

Jermaine lay perfectly still. His eyes swam behind his lids. "I'm in my apartment," he says in a dream-like speech. "I'm in my room, sitting on my chair in front of my bed. Watching TV. Watching the Knicks game. They're losing. I start to get mad that they're losing. I turn off the TV."

Doctor Carmichael is writing all this down. Suddenly she begins to feel cold. She looks up at the fan which seems to be going a lot faster than it had been before. The chain hits the light globe rapidly, mimicking the sound of someone about to give a toast at a wedding by hitting their metal knife on a wine glass. She looks back down at Jermaine and continues to listen.

"My friend Chico texts me. I get out of my chair and walk over to grab my phone that is lying at the head of my bed. As I'm reading his text the light in my room begins to flicker on and off until it goes off completely. My apartment tends to lose power every once and a while, but it only lasts for a few minutes. The lights never came back on that night. Then came this sound of something... thudding."

Doctor Carmichael looks at Jermaine with worry. She can see his chest heaving in and out heavily.

"I... I thought it was coming from my door, but when I went towards the front of my apartment the thudding stopped. I opened my door to see if anyone was there but the hallway was dark and empty. As I closed the door, I tried for the lights in my living room. It wouldn't come on. I walked back to my room when I heard that thumping again. *Thwump, Thwump, Thwump*. The thumps were slow and now it was coming from my bedroom. When I got to my room the thumping had become louder, coming... from outside my window. Something on the other side of my window was speaking. I thought it was impossible because I was on the fifth floor and... something was tapping my window and speaking. One word each time it hits."

Doctor Carmichael squinted her eyes, clearing her throat to ask, "And what word was that?"

Jermaine begins to breathe much faster now. His head turned from side to side very slowly. When he spoke it his breathing had started to slow, no longer speaking in his voice, but a much lower possessed voice instead. *"Bite, bite, bite."*

Doctor Carmichael's eyes grew wide and frantic. She began to feel much colder now. Placing her pen and pad on the table, she got to her feet to turn off the fan above, but as she looked up she noticed it was no longer spinning. The pull chain hung there still, untouched. Unbothered.

"The shades to my window were still down," Jermaine continued this time back to his normal voice. Doctor Carmichael slowly started to sit back down. Watching her client with a feeling of something that seemed a bit off. She was beginning to feel a bit creeped out, but she must help this man. Whatever it takes she must help this man. If she doesn't help him with this hypnosis, then his problems might become worse. Suicidally worse.

"I walked over cautiously to my window while the thumping began to go faster. I could hear my window begin to crack. I cry out 'Who's there!' The thumping had stopped. Suddenly I began to feel cold. I pulled the window shades up quickly and there was nothing there. The window didn't look cracked at all. As if there had been no thumping whatsoever, besides the *bite* of my heart."

Doctor Carmichael heard that odd voice again when he said the word *Bite*. Making her draw closer to Jermaine with her elbows on her knees, hands together almost like she would begin to say a prayer. "What happened next?" She says.

"The lights came back on," Jermaine said. "Nothing happened the rest of that night. I fell asleep. Except I woke up to use the restroom at two in the morning, that's when I saw... *it*."

Jermaine took a deep breath, shuddering as he exhaled the word *it*. Doctor Carmichael watched as a thin stream of air exited from his mouth. The room dropped a good ten degrees. She rubs her arms, feeling the goosebumps spread across her body. *Whatever it takes,* she thinks, reminding herself, *whatever it takes to make this man feel better.* But how truly freaked out she was starting to feel. Hearing that weird deep voice replaying in her head, over and over again. *Bite.*

"I stood there in the doorway to my room, watching this round object floating up and down in the corner of my room. I tried the lights. Nothing. As I moved into my room, it spoke to me."

"The head spoke to you?" Doctor Carmichael queries.

"Yes."

"What did it say?"

Jermaine lay there, slowly breathing now. He took a deep breath and began to speak in that new low tone of voice again. "Did you know a head can stay conscious for more than three minutes after it has been decapitated? There is no pain. Just a small bite, bite, *Bite! Did you know that, Doctor Carmichael?*" Jermaine bellows in his new voice.

Doctor Carmichael jumps to her feet. She could now begin to feel her heart racing. This has started to get too much for her, ready to call it quits. As she licked her lips to begin to say the two words to break Jermaine from his hypnosis, there came a soft tapping from the other side of her window. Her head quickly turns. The shades were still open, exposing the night that now lingers on. Yet, there was something else behind her shades that she could see. Something that is tapping on the other side.

Something floating.

The chain pull string clinked once above. Doctor Carmichael looks towards her ceiling fan. The chain danced a jig up and down before settling back down. The doctor blinks. She returns her gaze towards the window, now slightly starting to see a ball of some sort. The shades were still open to only see the object in question in strips. The ball hits the window, making Doctor Carmichael jump. When it hits the window again there Allison could see a wide set of eyes looking piercingly at her.

"Let me out," Jermaine whispers in his new voice.

Now having enough of this foolishness, Doctor Carmichael walks on over to the window. She grabs the cord for the blinds and pulls down on it. The shades go up quickly. Nothing behind her window except for a warm bright night in New York City. Doctor Carmichael scoffs. Feeling her muscles that she didn't know were tensing up started to relax a bit. Her shoulders begin to slouch. Her jaw starts to unhinge. She pulls down the blinds and closes the shades. When she turns back around to head back to her seat she pauses. Her eyes immediately saw something in the corner of her office, straight ahead from where Jermaine lay. She begins to feel her heart begin to race, feeling it pulse in her temple. Her mouth begins to hang agape, staring, not being able to move a single muscle as she begins to tense up yet again.

It was the head of an older man facing the upper corner of the office. Its skin is a foggy gray with thin balding hair that looks to be slicked back. A shadow had been cast to where it floated to show it had a long nose that resembled a witch. The veins hung down from the neck like exposed wires. The head slowly begins to turn towards Doctor Carmichael and Jermaine, then stops. Exposing its long nose and eyes that were a bloody orange. A smile protrudes from the corner of the head's mouth. As the mouth of the head begins to open so does Jermaine's mouth as he is still laid in his hypnotic trance.

"Thank you for letting me out, Doctor Carmichael," The floating head and Jermaine said in perfect unison, *"because of you diving into this man's head, I am free."*

The head and Jermaine begin to cackle. Doctor Carmichael ran back to where Jermaine lay. Sliding as she got to her knees next to Jermaine's ear. As she started to open her mouth, ready to speak the two words to bring him out of his trance to send this ungodly thing back from where it came from, she would only meet her demise.

"Angle's Hon-" Was all the doctor could speak.

"*Bite!*" The head yelled.

Before the doctor could utter the last syllable to break Jermaine's trance the bottom of her jaw slid right off her head. There had been no pain, just a lot of blood. The doctor tried to stifle a crying scream but all that came out was just a soft gurgle. Her tongue lulled to her neck. She looks down at her jaw that was on the floor instead of being attached to her head. As she gets to her feet her world begins to sway in and out. The head at the corner of the room begins to descend towards the Doctor. Doctor Carmichael steps away from Jermaine. She begins to head toward the door drunkenly, then trips on her own feet. Her breathing begins to become staggered. As she turns to her back she sees the veins of the floating head right above her very eyes.

The head begins to rotate downwards. It had a wicked smile that stretched from ear to ear. Its long witch-like nose nearly grazes the bridge of Doctor Carmichael's nose. The bloody orange eyes were big, wide, and full of satisfaction. The doctor lay there trying her best to utter the words 'Angle's Honey' but not having the slightest luck. A pool of blood begins to form around the doctor's head as she stares into the floating head's eyes.

"*Bite!*" The head says

Doctor Carmichael's neck snaps savagely to the side. She lay there with blood still oozing out of her mouth and eyes wide open. The head floats back up. It glances over to Jermaine who will lay there while he is stuck having the same dream over and over until his time will come, just as it did with Doctor Carmichael's.

The head begins to laugh methodically as it floats towards the window, phasing through it as if nothing was there at all, and makes its way out into New York to have a little fun. Just a little fun (*BITE*) to keep the heads rolling.

THE WORMS

EVERY TIME I DREAM I CAN HEAR IT, inching its way towards me. I never see it move, but I know it's getting closer. I know. This all started about three days ago, after a big hurricane nearly blew my beach house away. The city of Galveston had issued a city-wide evacuation. To grab all your family and possessions that you didn't want to see float down Highway 290. Except, I decided to stay. Why would I leave? I love stormy weather. It makes it the perfect opportunity to get some well-deserved writing done. And yet, I think about it to this day if I had made a mistake. If I had just left with the rest of the people off this island, maybe I wouldn't be going through this terrible nightmare.

The first night was not as bad, but it was building up to be one hell of a storm. The wind gushed over fifty miles an hour. I watched from my beach house, which had a good football field and a half lengths away from the beach, as the tides ripped madly at the beach wall with waves crashing high. Lightning struck far off in the distance as the sky was a violent purple. There was no thunder as of yet but I watched from the deck of my house with a cigarette in one hand and a glass of whiskey in the other.

Watching the storm grow closer with rage as the smell of salt water stenched the air around me. It started to rain which wasn't a problem until the rain turned into pebble-sized hail. When I got myself off the couch that sat on my upper deck I went inside, the hail started to come down even harder, now the size of ping pong balls. I could hear the thunder as the storm was now approaching much faster. I went downstairs and into the den to turn on the TV and see what the news was blabbering about now. As I turned the TV on it immediately shut right back off along with the power to my beach house. I listened and could hear the wind now howling outside. Making me think that an army of ghosts was outside my door and wanted to know if I had heard about our lord and savior. It wasn't total darkness in my home but it was enough that I needed to take out my phone to use the flashlight.

I looked at the screen of my phone which had a picture of me and my wife, Nancy, when we took our trip to Paris four years ago. Three months later after that trip, while we sat through a hurricane just like the one I'm sitting through now, I would wake up in bed to find Nancy had passed away in her sleep. Her autopsy showed that she had a brain aneurysm that killed her immediately. After I found out about that, I couldn't believe it. I didn't want to believe it. Before she died she would tell me about these dreams she would have. In them, these worms were swarming on top of a casket. She said she didn't know it was a casket until the night before she died.

"I can hear them," Nancy had told me the night before she died. "I can hear them slithering all around that casket. They sounded like Rice Krispy cereal after you pour the milk into it. How it sounds like it sizzles in the bowl of milk. And it just kept getting louder. I wanted to scream but somehow I knew that if I opened my mouth I would vomit out worms or they would just crawl into my mouth. The worms, Jackson. The worms are in my head."

She was completely distraught. After she told me about her dream she started to cry. I have never, in the sixteen years she and I have been together, seen her look so scared in my life. I held her that night, and if I knew it would have been the last night I would spend time with her in this realm of existence I would have held on to her tighter. Never wanting to let her go.

I miss her so much. I miss her long dark auburn hair. Her smooth skin with tiny freckles on her arms and chest. Her lips. Her dark brown eyes. The way she had to stand on her tiptoes to kiss me. I miss her so much. Four years have gone by without her touch. Four years of living my life without her by my side. Four years of hearing her last words play in my head like a broken record.

The worms are in my head.

The storm was now upon Galveston, just as powerful as it was four years ago. Lightning blared and thunder roared. The hail had stopped but the rain was now coming down with much gusto. The beach house made loud groaning noises as the wind pushed against my domain.

I went into the kitchen to look for some candles. Nancy always used to keep the candles in the pantry on a little shelf all to themselves. I thought it was a weird place to set your candles, but after she died I started to notice I picked up some of her habits. I took three Yankee candles out. I set one in the kitchen, one in the den, and one upstairs in my bedroom. I looked out the window after lighting the candle to see the rain had completely stopped. As if the eye of the storm was right above me. The calmness was eerie.

I went back outside to the deck and could feel the air pressure had dropped tremendously. Growing up around the beach kind of gives you an insight into how the weather would turn out. And at that moment I knew we were in for something nasty. Watching as lightning continued to pierce the ocean far off in the distance. Beginning to start heading back inside when something caught my eye. On the floor of my deck, closest to the door which leads inside, was a long earthworm. It was bright pink and had to be at least ten centimeters long. It slithered its way toward my door as if he was trying to get out of this hectic storm. I lifted my foot, ready to step on the creepy crawly then stopped. My foot hovered over the earthworm as I started to have a thought. Or maybe it was a weird premonition. Was stepping on a worm considered bad luck? I thought I had heard this before in a book or some movie, but whether it was something I heard or just a really weird intuition, I decided not to step on it. A cold shiver went up and down my spine, as I watched the worm lift its head, or maybe it was its butt, I couldn't tell and gave me what I came to believe to be a small nod. I went back inside and closed the door quickly, expecting to find the worm trying its best to come inside with me.

I went back downstairs to the den. My laptop sat on the table where I ate my home-cooked meals. After opening and logging in my laptop showed it was fully charged. I sat in the chair in front of my laptop. I opened my word processor which still had the novel I had been writing about of a man who was a lawyer and was being admitted to a crime to which he did not commit. I was about halfway finished with it and would work on it until the battery in my laptop died or whenever the power to my house would come back on. Whichever came first. My deadline was still months away to have this story completed, but after the death of my wife, I needed something to help distract me from thinking about her.

But was it her I was trying to forget? Or was it what she said right before she died I was trying to forget? The worms.

The battery life on my laptop was nearly diminished so I decided to stop there for the evening and try to get some sleep. The rain had started back up again about halfway through my laptop's battery life and hasn't eased up since. I shut my laptop. Stretching my arms and back then noticing something on the ceiling next to the fan. And it was moving. I got out of my chair to move the table over. I placed the chair I was in under the ceiling fan, and got on top. With my phone in my hand I turned the flashlight on. I stood at a good six feet and four inches so reaching for the ceiling was no problem. The problem was that when I shined the light of my phone on the ceiling I noticed it was another earthworm. Or perhaps it was the same one I saw back outside. I reached up and grabbed it with my hand not holding my phone.

I haven't held a worm in my hand since my father and I went fishing when I was only sixteen years old. That was nearly seventeen years ago. Yet there was something odd as I held the worm in my fingers. It started to squirm around in my hand. As if to tell me, *Unhand me, you scoundrel!* I stepped off the chair, making my way towards my front door to throw it outside into the storm. I opened the door to get ready to chunk my unwanted visitor out of my house when I looked into my hand to see the worm was no longer there. My eyes grew wide, feeling highly confused. I know I couldn't have dropped it, I would have felt it. Checking my clothes to see if it got stuck to my pants or the bottom of my shirt but still nothing.

I retraced my steps as lightning danced across the sky with its brother thunder two stepping behind. There was no trace of the worm. Nothing at all. I scratched my head and shrugged. Claiming that it was time for some sleep.

I went upstairs to start getting undressed and ready for bed. I stripped down to my tighty whities, got under my covers, and watched the storm come barreling in from my unshaded windows. As I closed my eyes I was out immediately.

I didn't dream that night, or so I thought. I woke up around 4 in the morning to use the restroom. The storm outside still sounded like a battle of the gods was raging on. When I walked into my bathroom which was attached to my bedroom, I flipped the lights on, lifted the toilet seat, and stared into the toilet bowl. Three more earthworms were slithering around in my toilet. They swam around, almost seeming like they were trying to connect to make one big circle. I started to feel cold and sick looking at those worms so I decided to flush them down the toilet. I peed, washed my hands, and went to lay back down, but started hearing my wife's voice in my head.

Jackson, Nancy said in my head. My eyes sprang open. I looked around my room, breathing heavy as if I would soon see her ghost, yet there was no one there. I heard her again saying, *The worms are mad.*

She said nothing more and after hearing that I couldn't fall back asleep. I sat up in bed, watching how the lightning lit up my room. I reached over to my nightstand. On top was a picture of Nancy standing against a tree with her hand holding her wrist; her other hand was shaped like a gun as she posed like one of Charlie's Angels. Next to the picture frame was a small lamp. I tried it to see if the power had come back on but, still nothing. So instead, I grabbed my tiny notebook which I have kept next to the bed since I can remember. I tend to get really good ideas at night so I write them down so I won't forget the next day.

I flipped a few pages until I came up with a blank one. I opened the drawer on my nightstand and fished out a pen. I jotted down what Nancy said to me in that paranormal kind of voice, *The Worms are mad…* I squinted my eyes in the dark to read those four words over and over again. I started to ponder on this, thinking about why would I hear my dead wife's voice telling me about these damn worms. Maybe she was trying to hint that I needed to call an exterminator. Or maybe...

I closed my notebook and sat it down back on my nightstand along with the pen I used. I rubbed my eyes and the bridge of my nose which caused me to yawn deeply. I was finally starting to feel tired again. I lay down and didn't wake up until six hours later.

When I woke up the rain had not stopped. After getting dressed I walked downstairs and noticed the ceiling fan was spinning making the den nice and cool. The power had come back on. I went to my couch, on the armrest was the remote. I grabbed it, turned the TV on, and only got a warning which read: *Category three hurricane warning issued for Galveston Island for the next two days.*

I flipped the channel to the local broadcast only to get the same message. Watching the news was out of the question so I decided to turn it off. I went over to Nancy's old record player. Below it were records she used to collect. I pulled out an Al Green record, set it on the record player, placed the needle on the vinyl, and then hit play. The song to play was *Take Me To The River*. I cranked it all the way up then started to do a little dance as I made my way to the kitchen to make myself some breakfast.

When I looked at the clock on the wall it read 10:30AM. I usually don't sleep late which is why my stomach could not stop growling. I cooked myself some eggs, bacon, sausage, and two pieces of toast with butter. When I finished cooking I sat down at the table in the chair that was facing the window which gave me a good view of not just the storm but the raging waves of the Gulf of Mexico.

The rain was light but the clouds looked darker than ever. It wasn't the violent purple I saw but more of a calmer violet. Lightning flashed in the clouds, not once striking down on the island. I could hear the wind pushing against my house and heard it groaning as if it was trying its best not to collapse on top of me. This house has survived many hurricanes and I was sure it could survive this one. Below my house the rain was causing it to flood, meaning I was stuck here until the storm cleared up.

As I took my plate to the sink to let it soak before I cleaned it completely I started to hear the AL Green record start to slow and become disoriented until it finally came to a stop. My house was now deathly quiet minus the rain that was beginning to pick back up. I dried my hands as I walked into the den. The needle of the record player was sticking far off to the side away from the vinyl. When I walked up to the vinyl player I hit the stop button, causing the record to stop revolving. I looked to my left of the record player and could feel a cold chill race across my body as I watched a worm crawl its way down the corner of the player. My blood began to boil as I tried to figure out how the hell these damn bugs keep seeping into my house.

Seeping. That was a funny way to put it. I felt like I was being invaded by these worms. I bent over to pick up the worm. It squirmed around between my thumb and index finger. This time I kept my eye on it to make sure I didn't lose sight of it as I took it to my front door. I opened my door with my eyes still on the worm and like a roid rage baseball pitcher I threw the worm across my yard and saw it made a tiny splash down below.

"And stay out," I said to the worm. Hoping that it is now drowning in the flood down below. Can worms drown? I didn't know and at the moment didn't care.

I walked back inside, thinking of how I might spend my day since there would be no chance of me taking my F-150 truck into town. I would eventually pull out one of my Ray Bradbury books and read until my eyes grew tired. I'd get a little more writing done until I heard Nancy's voice again. It made me think of what I heard her say last night. Then the notebook on my nightstand came into my head as well.

I closed my laptop, got out of my chair, proceeded upstairs, and stopped at my doorway dumbstruck. There had to be over fifty worms crawling outside of my window. I almost felt sick to my stomach. My lip curled giving me an Elvis Presley look when I saw my reflection in my dresser mirror. I crept cautiously into my room, up to my window, staring at the worms that nearly covered my entire bay window. I tapped on the window where the worms slithered around, almost as if trying to avoid the rain. Out of all the times I wished I had a few seagulls on my deck this was the only time.

I turned towards my nightstand and walked over to it. I picked up my notebook and flipped to the page I had written last night. I stared at the page I wrote on and... couldn't believe my eyes. I know for a damn fact that last night I wrote what I could hear Nancy tell me; *The Worms are mad*. But as I read what was on that page was not what I wrote down. The writing on the page looked nothing like my handwriting at all. On the page read; *We are mad.*

I shivered as lightning cracked the sky followed by heavy thunder booming, causing my house to tremble a little. I flipped through the pages to see if anything else was written but there was nothing else. I turned back to my bay window to see the worms had stopped moving. As if they had all hibernated while being stuck to my window. I scratched my head thinking about what was going on.

"Nancy," I said to the empty room, "are you there?"

But all I got in return was the silence of my beach house along with the storm going on outside. What was I thinking anyway? That the voice of my dead wife was going to answer me and say, *yes honey I'm here*. Instead, I walked back downstairs to make myself a strong glass of whiskey to try and help me think about how to deal with these worms.

After I poured myself a glass I started to head back upstairs to get another look at my window. When I reached my room I stopped yet again at my doorway and let the glass of whiskey slip out of my hands, shattering all over the floor as I looked at my window which was perfectly clean and not a single worm in sight. I stepped over the broken glass into my room and walked over to my window. I got down onto my knees to make sure they all didn't just fall off onto my deck and yet there was still nothing. Was I beginning to lose my mind? I could have sworn on my life that there were over fifty worms on my window and now there's not a single one. I checked to see if there were any holes or some sort of entrance that these worms were coming through but I saw nothing, zilch, nada.

I got back up to my feet, staring off into the storm that was progressively getting worse. I waited for Nancy to come back into my head, but just like my bay window, there was nothing there.

I spent the rest of that day peering over my shoulders expecting to see a worm crawling on me. I scratched my head so much that I could feel my scalp burning. I cleaned up my shattered glass from my doorway then made another glass of whiskey. I sat at the table in silence for nearly two hours. When I got up from the table, I made myself something quick to eat. But when I finished cooking and sat down at the table my stomach twisted and turned. As a writer, my imagination started filling my brain with what could be inside my peanut butter jelly, and banana sandwich. I started picturing maggots squirming around after I would take that first bite. Feeling them wiggle around in my mouth as they were cut in half by my teeth. Having them slowly crawl back up my throat as I tried to swallow.

I pushed the sandwich to the side, no longer hungry. I took one big chug of my whiskey and started to feel tired and drained. I looked at the clock which only read 4 in the afternoon. I got up from my table and made my way towards the den. I plopped down on the couch and grabbed my remote to see if I could get anything on the television. The local channel still had the national weather broadcast warning. I flipped through more channels and came across a show my wife loved to watch called Naked and Afraid. A show about people surviving in the wilderness while being completely nude. My eyes started to feel heavy and I could feel sleep ready to take over my body. I didn't refuse and drifted off into a deep sleep.

I dreamed that I was in a bright white room. I started to hear something behind me. However, what stood in front of me had me more baffled than what was going on behind me. Standing in front of me was Nancy. She wore the same outfit we buried her in. A silk red dress with flat black shoes. Her sleek black hair went down to her back and her skin looked more pale than what I remembered.

"What's going on Nancy?" I said.

She said nothing.

"Where am I?"

Still nothing, but she did start to smile.

"Tell me about the.." *Worms* was what I wanted to say but felt a restriction of saying that particular word.

The noise I heard coming from behind me grew louder yet I still did not turn around.

"Dammit Nancy, speak to me!"

Nancy opened her mouth and hundreds of worms started creeping out of her mouth. A good pile of them made an audible splat as it hit the ground and more worms started coming out of her mouth. The worms started crawling towards me. The noise behind me started to crescendo in volume. More and more worms flooded out of Nancy's mouth and some were starting to come out of her ears. Before I woke up she finally spoke to me. In a voice that was too deep for hers. A voice that was too deadly for hers.

"The worms," Nancy said, "are in the house. And soon will be in you."

Nancy raised her hands towards me, outstretched towards me. Her body was becoming consumed by the worms waking me out of that nightmare as I screamed myself awake.

I sat on my couch as the TV was still playing. Now on to a different show than what I had been previously watching before. The rain was coming down much harder now. I wiped my forehead to find I was sweating madly. I checked my phone and saw I had been asleep for three hours. My stomach was hurting from not eating anything since this morning, and after that horrible nightmare, I wasn't sure I would be able to eat.

But instead, I was able to eat. I cooked myself a burger and scarfed it down in no time. I went upstairs to get a shower to wash away the stench of whiskey sweat off me. I got out, dried off, put on some comfy night clothes, and was beginning to head downstairs to get some writing done when I stopped at the bottom step. My mouth hung ajar, as I saw the entire floor of my den was covered with earthworms. The smell of dirt and soil was foul. I couldn't move. I couldn't think. Why was this happening?

I went back upstairs to grab my phone. I unlocked it and started to call an exterminator. But what good was that gonna do, I thought to myself. The roads are probably closed and by now every exterminator in town must now be on the other side of Houston. I decided I would leave a message. The phone rang only twice before a burly-sounding man came on to tell me to leave a voice message and that he would get back to me ASAP. I started to record my message as I made my way back downstairs and again stopped at the bottom step.

The worms were gone. As if they were never there to begin with. What the hell was going on? I was furious. I walked all around the bottom half of my house to make sure there were no worms and came up with nothing. I had forgotten that I was leaving a message for an exterminator as the call was still going. A robotic woman had said my time was up for leaving a message that made me jump. I looked at my phone, hung up, and sat my phone next to my laptop on the table. I didn't want to stay here much longer. Maybe I should have gotten out of here before the storm got worse.

The worms are in the house, my dream Nancy had told me, *and now they are in you.*

I scratched my head hard enough that it started to sting. I looked at my fingernails and saw small traces of blood. I didn't even want to write anymore. I didn't want to do anything. I went over to the window in my den and looked outside.

The storm was not easing up a bit. The wind must have been blowing a good 60 miles an hour. The rain came down slanted and lightning struck down from the dark clouds with thunder roaring loud enough to shake my beach house. The ground was covered with water that probably came up to my knees. There is no way I'm getting out of here. None at all.

Part of me was tired and the other part wouldn't even try to comprehend sleeping. So I did the next best thing. I went to the kitchen and started to grab one of my glasses for my whiskey. I paused, then closed the cabinet door. I picked up the bottle of Jack Daniel's, unscrewed the cap, lifted the bottle to my lips, and took three huge swigs. My throat was satisfyingly burning, feeling it go all the way down to my chest, then finally settling into my stomach.

I walked back upstairs to just watch the storm from the foot of my bed with the bottle still in my hand. An hour passed and there was less than a quarter left of my whiskey when I just started drinking it was only halfway empty. The room spun around me as my eyes grew heavy. I sat the bottle down at the foot of my bed and then laid down. Staring up at the roof as I listened to the rain pummel against my house. My eyes shut as I listened… listened… silence.

When I opened my eyes I noticed the rain had stopped but not just that I couldn't breathe. I felt as if I was suffocating. My eyes were open but everything looked dark. I tried lifting my arms, legs, and head but felt they were being restrained down. I could feel long tiny bodies slither on top of me. Trying to enter any orifice into my body. I wiggled my shoulders and was starting to finally break free. I pushed my head forward and it came out on top of what I discovered to be hundreds of earthworms on top of me. I screamed. Many of the worms tried to enter my mouth as I was struggling to get up. I wriggled my shoulders until they too were above the worms and pushed myself off the bed. I fell flat on my face which made me see stars. I shook my head then without missing a beat flipped over to my back and scooted far away from the bed. I looked to see I knocked over my bottle of whiskey and noticed my bed was empty. There were no worms on there and I felt as if I was going insane. Or perhaps maybe I already have.

The storm outside was now calm. The eye of the hurricane was now hovering above my house. Everything was still and quiet. I got to my feet, still a little drunk but it wasn't enough to where the room was still spinning. I swiped away at my body, thinking I could still feel the worms crawling all around me. I could still hear how they would slither with their slimy bodies, grooving against one another and my body. I can hear them. As if the worms are...

No, I thought to myself, no, no, no. I ran downstairs and stopped at the bottom step. A cold shiver went down my body and goosebumps went down the nape of my neck. Dead center in the den was a casket. It slowly opened and thousands of earthworms came barreling out. Then a loud cracking sound started protruding from the casket. An arm reached out of the casket and I could see it was a woman's arm. A gold wedding ring glimmered as the lightning flashed across the sky.

"*Jaaacksooon,*" the being in the casket bellowed. "*The worms Jackson. The worms are mad. We are mad. They want you Jackson. They want to feast on your decomposing flesh until you're nothing more than bones for the maggots. You should have left the island. You should have taken me off the island, so that I can still breathe the air you still breathe. But you killed me. And now my worms will drive you into insanity!*"

The worms slithered quickly towards my feet. I couldn't move and I was paralyzed. Weighed down as heavy as the guilt I had for not leaving the island sooner with my wife. The worms started to crawl onto my feet and raced their way up my body. I screamed and as I did the worms entered my mouth, entered my ears, my nose, my eyes, and then...

I sat up from my bed screaming and gasping for air. Once I fully caught my breath I screamed and kept screaming as I could still hear the sound of worms slithering all around me. Finally understanding what my wife was speaking about before she died. Even after she died I was still picking up her habits. I screamed because I knew that the worms were now in *my* head.

ABNORMAL

"UH OH," ANGELA SAID, who is currently eight and a half months pregnant, grabbing hold of her stomach as water rushed down between her legs. "Eddie, I think it's time." She gets up from the dinner table where the two were engaged in a five thousand-piece jigsaw puzzle of a modern Rome painting. Eddie rushed to her side and helped her walk to the front door. He grabs the keys off the key hook and walks his pregnant wife to the car.

He helps her into the car, reminds her about her breathing techniques, and rushes back into the house to gather some supplies they'll need while they are at the hospital. Eddie tosses some clean clothes and their phone chargers in a bag along with toothbrushes and other necessities the couple will need.

Eddie rushes back to the car as his wife is doing her breathing techniques. She gave out a *Hee Hee Ho* and then screamed a bloody murder kind of scream as the contractions were getting closer. Eddie begins to drive towards Cox Medical Center Hospital and they have to stop at a red light. If given the choice he would have taken her to Mercy Hospital up in Springfield - only because that's where he was born - but the Cox Medical Center was the closest and even their primary doctor suggested the facility and who wants to argue with a doctor. The traffic light still glowing red made Eddie feel uneasy.

"Come on you stupid light," Eddie said.

Angela is still doing her *Hee Hee Ho* breathing and rubbing her belly in a circular motion. She let out another scream as she pushed her stomach upwards and pushed on her seat with her arms. The light then turns green. Eddie put his hazard lights on and began to go twenty over the speed limit. The pain slowly faded as Angela went back to her breathing. She rubs her stomach and notices that something is wrong.

"Eddie," Angela said, "Please hurry, something doesn't feel right anymore." Her skin turned pale and a cold sweat began trickling down the side of her face. Eddie could see the horror in her expression and rushed to the hospital.

When they pulled up Eddie began to honk his car horn to have some nurses come and assist them. One nurse came out with a wheelchair and another nurse opened the door to help Angela out of the car and onto the wheelchair.

"Please, please," Angela said frantically. "I think there's something wrong with my baby!"

The two nurses looked at each other with a worrisome expression, rushing Angela inside.

They got her into a room, helped remove her clothes into a gown, laid her on the bed, and propped open her legs as a doctor walked in ready to deliver a baby.

"How are we doing today?" The doctor asked.

Angela shrieked in pain and told the doctor that there was an odd feeling going on and is worried about the baby.

The doctor sat down in front of Angela's vagina and noticed a head beginning to crown.

"Yep, we have a baby making its way into the world." The doctor said, "Alright Mrs. Lewis I'm going to need you to take three quick breaths and push as hard as you can."

She did as the doctor ordered and as she pushed the head of the newborn began sprouting out. That's when the doctor made a terrible discovery. The newborn was being choked to death by its umbilical cord. Not knowing how long this was going on the doctor asked the nurse to quickly hand him surgical scissors. He carefully cut the umbilical cord from the infant's neck and as he did the infant's body slid out of the mother's womb and out to the doctor's arms as he held a lifeless body.

"What's wrong," Angela said, looking frantically around as sweat began running over her eyes, "is my baby alright?"

The doctor took the body of the newborn into another room and began to perform CPR. The infant gave no sign of life for about fifty-nine seconds until it gave a choking cough and began crying. The doctor sighed in relief as he picked up the baby and took him back to his mother.

Angela on the verge of a breakdown started bawling as the doctor walked in with her newborn son and handed him to his mother.

"He gave us quite a scare," the doctor said, "his umbilical cord was wrapped around the little guy's throat and to be quite honest with you, it's a miracle he survived."

The words *it's a miracle he survived* causes Angela to cry even harder as Eddie walks into the delivery room and rushes to her side.

"Mr. Lewis, I had just informed your wife about a small dilemma we came across during the delivery."

"Is it bad?" Eddie said with concern in his voice.

"It could have been a lot worse," the doctor started as he walked up closer to the parents and observed the now-sleeping child. "No telling how long he was being choked before I cut the umbilical cord, but," He paused and looked at the new parents with a look that scared Eddie a bit. "With a lack of oxygen it was receiving and having to perform CPR on a newly infant, his brain function may develop some abnormal qualities."

"What do you mean by abnormal, doc?" Eddie asked.

"Well, when a child has little to no oxygen while being born we have what is called Cerebral Hypoxia which refers to a brain starving for oxygen. Thanks to medical research we now have access to give your child all the help it needs."

The last statement brought ease to the parents as they looked at their bundle of joy resting as it dreamed and spreading his pink, thin fingers.

"You hear that?" Angela whispered, smiling at her son, "You're going to be just fine. My little Raymond."

***

The leaves began to turn a Golden brown and a sunny red, gracefully spilling to the ground. The wind whistled in the chilling air of a tune that fall had arrived. Angela hastily caught up on a late spring cleaning of the house as Raymond slept peacefully in his crib. She knew that she could complete the bottom half of the house with the dusting and the mopping and all that jazz. She also hopes she could get a quarter of the upper half - only if Raymond is still asleep - somewhat cleaned to finish up the next day. This weekend Eddie promised he would finally tackle the gutters.

He promised.

Eddie works as a high school Principal, who would someday hope to become Superintendent of his district. All the students adored Principal Lewis and the teachers admired him. He was the kind of man who could look you in the eyes and have every lie detained and every truth spat out, but also he was a soft-spoken man.

Angela worked as a substitute teacher when she met Eddie and he was teaching Senior Calculus at Branson High. While on their lunch break, they bumped into each other causing Angela to drop the warm papers she had printed for her lessons. They both apologized as they bent down to gather the scattered papers their hands touched each other and stared deeply into each other's eyes. They kind of shit you'd see in a Rom-Com only it was real and there was no audience to laugh at the clumsy couple.

Now Angela, being a stay-at-home mom has put her in a new world she had been desperately waiting for.

Motherhood.

As she carries a bucket of water with a mop bouncing in it with each step Angela takes going up the stairs she begins to hear Raymond crying, telling her that he was hungry. The child, now being four months old, almost had a schedule of when he would sleep, eat, and even shit going on for a few days. For several weeks there are days where he doesn't want to follow the schedule, leading to long restless nights, to a grumpy and sassy day.

This was going to be a grumpy-sassy kind of day.

Angela sets the bucket of water and mop in the upstairs bedroom that separates her and Eddie's bedroom and Raymond's. She shuffles into her child's room and picks him up as he still cries and begins to rock him gently with a soft, *Shh Shh Shh,* heading back downstairs. His crying lasted until Angela sat him down in a high chair. The last bit of tears strolled down his cheeks and his face was enlightened as she brought out a banana-flavored Gerber baby meal with his Mickey Mouse plastic spoon.

Raymond is picked up out of his high chair once he is finished eating and carried over to the freshly cleaned living room which still has a strong scent of lavender and pine sol. He sat in his baby bouncer that was placed a good nine feet away from the TV which was showing Sesame Street, but had already become preoccupied with the mobile that hung a star, a teddy bear, and a moon.

"Be a good boy for mommy while she gets some cleaning done," Angela told her son.

As she turned around to head towards the stairs Raymond began to bounce around in his seat and uttered the word, MA, loud enough that Angela stopped at the bottom of the stairs and slowly turned around to look at the infant trying to grab the moon from the mobile. She looks around as if she had someone to confirm what she heard, or maybe what she thought she heard.

She walks back into the room and bends over, getting to an eye-to-eye level with her son.

"Did you say," Angela licks her lips, "Mama?"

She knew she had to be crazy to think that a child only 4 months old to say 'mama', but then she remembered about the doctor after giving labor that he might be born with abnormal behaviors.

The boy now, who was trying to chew on his foot like a dog with a really bad itch on his ankle, slowly releases his foot and stares his mother in her eyes. He cocks his head to the right and blinks twice slowly.

"Muh-Muh." Raymond started to babble.

Angela's eyes became ecstatic and she gave a wild smile.

"Muh-Muh-Muh," Raymond began to say, "Muh-Muh Mama."

All the blood rushed to Angela's face as she wanted to scream in joy but figured that might scare the baby. Instead, she began to laugh hysterically which also caused Raymond to start bellowing out in laughter.

This is insane! Angela thought. *He's only a few months old and he knows how to say mama! I might have given birth to the next Einstein!*

Raymond was still giggling as Angela picked up her child and began laughing along with him. Raymond gave out a small, *Heh-hehe,* and Angela mimicked his laughter tickling his stomach. But Raymond then stopped laughing and looked at his mother with a stone face, giving Angela a small chill. The room fell silent with the sounds of cars passing through the neighborhood, on their way to pick up the kids from school. Raymond, not blinking or moving a single muscle.

Angela sits him back in his chair and Raymond doesn't even take his eyes off her still.

"Mama," Raymond said in a whispery rasp, "why do you mock me?"

Angela could feel her body grow colder and slowly stood straight up, and it was Angela now not taking her eyes off Raymond. She begins to walk backward slowly to the kitchen and as she does Raymond begins to attack his foot again giving it a big ol chomp with his gums, gooing and gawing away.

When Angela makes it into the kitchen she goes for her phone that was sitting on the kitchen counter charging. She unlocks it and scrolls through her contacts until she finds Eddie's name and proceeds to call him. It rang four times and by the fifth time, he answered it.

"Hey, honey," Eddie said. "Everything okay?"

"Well," Angela paused and thought about what she was going to say to make it not sound as ridiculous as it was. "Something happened with Raymond earlier."

"Is he alright?" Eddie said with a strict concern in his voice.

"Everything is fine, he's fine. It's just… Raymond said mama just a few minutes ago."

There was a brief silence between the two on the phone as Angela could hear Eddie breathing on the other side.

"He probably just said it in his baby talk. You know, like mashing up words with him even knowing it."

"That's what I thought too but then he said more." Angela's voice now sounds a bit paranoid.

"What do you mean he said more?"

"After he said that he said-" Before she could finish Raymond began crying again letting her know that he was tired and ready to go to bed.

"I have to go. I'll talk to you when you get home." She hung up the phone and went back into the living room where Raymond was red in the face and exhausted

She picks him up and looks at him, waiting to see if he'll speak again but doesn't. She shakes her head and takes her bawling son back up to his room for a nap.

A grumpy and sassy day indeed.

***

Eddie sat in traffic and began to ponder on the conversation he had with his wife. He could hear the off-putting tone that set Eddie baffled. His mind winding up tighter, creating a small tension headache - that would slowly turn into a migraine - until he released the anaconda death grip he had

36

locked on his steering wheel with his hands, and felt the rapid pulse beating away on his palms.

He pulled down his sun visor and stared at the photograph that was stuck on there by two pieces of scotch tape, one on the bottom and the other on top. It was a photo of the couple on their Honeymoon at Niagara Falls a day after their wedding.

He reminisces about the sweet passionate night before taking a tour of one of the seven wonders of the world. A few months later they found out that they were expecting to have a baby.

Then everything changed, and not for the better.

The small tension headache began rapping on his temple impetuously now. The car behind him in a small Honda Accord honked at Eddie - letting him know he wanted to get out of there just as fast as you too, buddy.

Eddie inhales sharply and drives forward as traffic begins to move forward like a creek when the sticks have been removed one by one. Eddie passed what had caused the bumper-to-bumper traffic at the busiest time of the day.

A small Kia had flipped over, laying on its roof and a Dodge Ram truck engine had caught on fire. Two paramedic trucks were parked on the side next to the flipped car and a firetruck slowly came to a stop and parked close to the burning truck. A pair of paramedics were attempting to pull the man out of the truck who was bleeding from the head - later in the news they would report that the man had died of a major brain injury - and another pair of paramedics trying to restrain a black woman in a bright yellow dress. She had cuts on her arms and beads of blood raced down to her hand. She had a black eye and a small gash on her upper lip.

"MY BABY!" The woman shouts loud enough for Eddie to hear her as he slowly passes her in the steady stream of traffic. "GOD WILL SOMEONE PLEASE GET MY BABY OUT OF MY CAR!"

The paramedics finally get their strength in check, pulling her back away from the car. A fireman gets down on his stomach and begins to crawl into the flipped Kia cuts the baby loose from the car seat is brought out and rushes over to the back of one of the ambulances and later hears the woman cry out in vain as her child is dead.

The traffic finally gained momentum and Eddie proceeded forward and began to softly sob. He would have to wipe his tears and gather his thoughts together before pulling up to the driveway of his home and letting his wife see him crying again.

The tension headache was now a full-blown migraine.

***

The smell of chicken and dumplings began to mask the newly cleaned house (only the bottom half that is) along with steamed carrots and corn. Angela kept the baby monitor close to the stove so she could hear when Raymond woke up. The news was being streamed on Angela's iPad as the reports of two deaths due to a Dodge Ram hitting a Kia Soul caused it to hit the side rail on the highway and flip over. The driver of the Dodge Ram, thirty-seven-year-old David Nice was pronounced dead at the hospital along with 2-year-old Megan Birddy dead at the scene of the crash.

Angela locks her iPad as she is done listening to what's going on in today's depressing world. She then turns off the stove top burners to start preparing the table. When she turned around she was not ready to accept where her eyes gazed upon.

Raymond came through the kitchen doorway, walking. He stepped as if each tile on the floor were telling him which one to step on. Angela lets out a small scream that sends Raymond to lose his balance and falls flat on his ass and begins wailing.

"What the actual fuck!" Angela proclaimed.

Eddie, who just drove up the driveway and was making his way inside, heard Angela yelling and took off inside. He opens the door and in such a rush he leaves the door open letting the cool air in. He runs past the living room and into the kitchen to see Raymond crying on the floor and Angela - not even noticing Eddie - glaring at Raymond.

"What's wrong? Are you okay?" Eddie said as he picked up Raymond from the floor.

"Our son," she began to say trembling, "our son just walked right through the doorway.

Eddie stared at his wife with a puzzled look and looked at Raymond who had stopped crying and was now sucking on three of his right fingers. Bending over to pick Raymond up from the ground, Eddie let out a long sigh.

"Honey, you know that's not possible, right? Maybe you just imagine-"

"I know what the fuck I saw, Eddie!" Angela shouted.

"Calm down Angela." Eddie raised his hand slowly which wasn't holding Raymond. "Listen, sounds like you had a pretty rough day and I know for the past three nights you've been the one that's been getting up to put the baby back to sleep when he wakes up, you're tired and your mind is playing tricks on you."

"I know what I saw, I'm not crazy!"

"I didn't say that. Look I'll take over finishing making dinner and you just go upstairs and lay down for a bit. How does that sound?"

Angela stared at Eddie and then at Raymond. She could hear the sincerest in his voice and she remembered the man she married. The way he stood there, with the sheer vibrato of a man. Her face began to turn red as she started to sob softly. She sniffled and gave a weak smile.

"Yeah, okay," Angela said with a raspy tone. "Thank you, sweetheart." She walks up to him to hug him and kiss him as she heads upstairs.

"If you end up falling asleep I'll let you rest then wake you up so you can eat," Eddie said to his wife, as she began walking up the stairs. "And don't worry about Raymond, I can take care of him."

When she reached her bedroom she plopped down face first into her pillow and laid there listening to the sound of kitchenware musically strum as Eddie finished up making dinner and without a single thought she fell into a deep sleep.

She is later awoken by Eddie lightly knocking on the bedroom door. Her eyes were still adjusting as she turned over and looked at the clock. It read 8:14 PM on it. She had slept for nearly 3 hours.

"Jesus, Eddie," Angela said groggily. "Why'd you let me sleep for so long."

"I didn't," Eddie said. "I tried waking you up at 6:30 but you didn't even budge."

"Oh," Angela said as she sat up in bed and scratched the back of her head.

"I finally got Raymond to lay down, that stinker is a stubborn one. Um, I also wanted to ask you something, well two things to be frank." Eddie started.

Angela, still in the process of being awake, waves her hand to Eddie for him to speak.

"Have you been taking your medicine?"

She looked at him not saying a word, but instead having her eyes tell him, *Are you serious right now,* and let out a long-winded irritating sigh.

"Right of course you have." Eddie knew she was lying but he didn't want to rush into an argument. Especially after getting Raymond to sleep. "The other thing is, when you called me earlier, what did you mean Raymond said more? You know-"

"He said 'Why do I mock him'," Angela said without any hesitation.

An uncomfortable silence grew in the bedroom as Eddie's mind began to race. Everything that happened two years ago began to play in Eddie's mind as he blew out a dissatisfied breath.

"Are we seriously going to do this again?" Eddie said sternly.

"What are you talking ab-" Angela began to say before she was cut off.

"Stop acting like you don't remember, Angela. What happened two years ago didn't just hurt you but it hurt me t-"

Angela shot straight out of bed, pointed at Eddie, and looked at him with a sickening glare. There was static with her stare as the memories finally revealed their bastardly face. A small single tear came down her cheek.

"You promised," Angela hissed. "You promised you wouldn't bring that up ever again!" She walked closer to him, almost touching Eddie's nose with her own.

Eddie could feel another tension headache coming in like a steam train and backed away from Angela. She wiped away the tears and sat back down on the bed.

"I'm sorry." Angela whimpered

"Yeah," Eddie said. "I'll heat your dinner. It'll be ready in five." He turned around and walked out of the bedroom and downstairs to the kitchen.

Anglea laid back down with her feet hanging off the side of the bed and crossed her arms around her head to hold back her tears. A few seconds later there was a small scratching sound. It was like a small kitten running on wood floors. They were the sounds of quick footsteps running outside in the hallway close to the bedrooms. Anglea takes her arms off her face and begins to listen closely.

There came four quick steps approaching the bedroom door. Anglea shot up and watched her doorway. Her breaths were rapid and sharp. The footsteps stopped and everything fell silent except for the commotions coming from downstairs as Eddie was preparing her meal along with the sound of warm air escaping from her mouth. Her eyes wandered from the doorway to her closet- which was closed - and then back to the doorway. She calmed herself down and slowly laid back down. When the back of her head made contact with the bed she could feel a presence next to her. The smell of baby odor grew strong as she turned and saw Raymond lying next to her staring into her dark brown eyes.

"Mama," Raymond said horsily. "Mama, Daddy doesn't love you anymore."

Anglea wanted to scream in sheer terror but something was preventing her from even making a single sound. She dazed at her son with confusion and concern.

"How are you doing all this?" Anglea said softly.

"Daddy didn't want me to be born. Daddy wanted me not to be alive." Raymond crawled his way towards Anglea as she was paralyzed from moving. He softly bumps his head into her breast and begins to crease her face gently with his small stubby hands.

"Raymond, daddy and I love you." Anglea pleaded. "Please, you're scaring mommy."

"Mama," Raymond raised his head, again making eye contact with her. "Don't you love me?"

She began to cry and wrapped her arms around her child, rocked him gently, and shut her eyes. "Mommy's always going to love you."

Raymond bounced his head up and down and shook his body causing Anglea to stop rocking him.

"Kill Daddy," Raymond whispered.

Angela's eyes looked directly at the ceiling as terror began to grow stronger in her.

"Kill daddy." Raymond repeated, "Kill daddy, kill daddy, kill daddy!"

"No," Anglea softly said. "I won't do it!" She released her arms from around him to find that she was holding nothing at all and began to hear Raymond crying from his bedroom. Anglea shot up and looked around the room. She runs her fingers through her hair roughly.

What is going on? Anglea pondered as she got out of bed and went into Raymond's room. She saw the little boy in his crib crying and she picked him up. He stops crying immediately and Anglea waits for him to speak again, but he only utters the baby talk of gooing and gaaing. He rubs his hand gently down his mother's face and begins to giggle. Anglea smiles.

***

Eddie sat Angela's food on the table as she walked in holding Raymond. He turned and looked at her bemusingly. She sits him in his high chair and gives him one of his toys used for teething, and she takes her seat across from him.

"Need anything while I'm still up?" Eddie said.

"Glass of water, please," Anglea said not even taking her eyes off Raymond.

Eddie goes to the top shelf and grabs a glass then fills it with water. "I thought he was asleep?" Eddie said, bringing the glass of water to her.

"He was but he started crying when I was coming downstairs," Anglea said. The voice of Raymond saying, *Kill Daddy!*, replayed in her head making her heart beat faster and her hands began to shake.

When Eddie sat down at the table to Angela's right, she finally looked down at her food and began eating. First with the corn and carrots, then stuffing her face with the chicken and dumplings.

"Hungry?" Eddie asked with an amused smile.

Anglea nodded as she took a sip from her water. Her head began to feel fuzzy, like static from a TV that didn't have a good connection. Eddie was beginning to tell his day to Anglea but it all sounded muffled to her. The room slowly began to spin as she looked up at Raymond who was staring at her with a look that could cut diamonds.

Raymond's eyes began to retreat to the back of his head and began to convulse. Anglea knew it was all in her head because Eddie was still talking about his day. The room spun faster and faster making Angela feel like her dinner would come back up. Raymond's mouth began to open as a shadow figure began to crawl out of his mouth, but before the figure could fully emerge, Eddie noticed Angela hadn't been paying attention. He snapped his finger in front of her face and the room suddenly stopped spinning and Raymond was gumming away his toy.

"Did you even hear anything I said?" Eddie remarked.

"I'm sorry," Anglea said, rubbing her eyes and up to her temple. "Just have a lot on my mind and got a headache coming on."

"You too, huh? Well, why don't you just start getting ready for bed?" He helped clear the table and began washing her dishes.

Angela looked up back at Raymond and he began to yawn and rub his eye signaling that he was finally ready to go to bed. When she got out of her chair she felt almost in a trance. She shifted her weight over to her child and picked him up.

"I'll be up in a little bit hun," Eddie said, as he watched his wife pick up Raymond and take him upstairs. To him, her movements resembled that of a drunken person, but it was very precise. She didn't say a word as she picked up her child and walked out to their rooms.

The baby fell limp and cold in Angela's arms midway up the stairs. She looked down and his skin began to lose its color. Her eyes widened and stopped at the very top of the stairway. Raymond let out a small cough then stopped breathing. Angela screamed for Eddie but there was no audio, no vibration in the noise. She fell to her knees and the child stared up at her.

"He didn't want me to live," Raymond said but this time in a little girl's voice. As Angela was about to cry a spite of rage came upon her and she shot back up to her feet. Raymond then began to again yawn and gum away at his hand.

When the two reached Raymond's room she laid him down in his crib and pulled his blanket on top of him. The toddler then threw his hands in the air and Anglea bent down to kiss him on his forehead.

"I'm dying," the child whispered.

"Why?" Angela uttered. She felt the pure dread in the question as she already knew the answer.

Raymond's eyes steadily became heavy and he finally fell asleep. Anglea watched her son sleep, softly snoring.

Eddie came up behind her quietly and gently put his arm around her. "Come on, let's go lay down." And he guided her out of his room and towards their bedroom. Anglea looked back at Raymond who was still sleeping in his crib and she turned back around and went straight to the bed and laid down on top of the covers.

Eddie joined her on the bed after he took his clothes off and into his nightwear. He huddled up to Anglea, spooning her. He whispered in her ear 'Good Night.' and fell into a deep sleep.

Anglea stared at the wall, not even the slightest bit tired. She listened as Eddie began to snore and he turned over on his other side. Her mind was racing and she ended up making herself scared. She shuts her eyes in the hope of falling asleep.

Maybe all of this is a bad dream, She pondered. *Maybe if I close my eyes now, I'll wake up and none of this would have happened and Raymond wouldn't-*

The sound of scratching on the floor began to crescendo throughout the house. Anglea's eyes opened and her heart began to flutter. She tried to listen closely but Eddie's snoring made it impossible to hear anything. He took short and sharp breaths when he was asleep which sounded like a saw cutting a tree. Anglea carefully gets out of bed, walks to her doorway and peeks into the hallway.

The scratching sound now was scattering at the bottom half of the house. She walks out into the hallway and goes into Raymond's room only to find his crib is empty. Her breathing started turning into a whimper and she could hear the sound of silverware being clanged around and she turned and walked towards the stairway.

"Raymond," Anglea whispered as she slowly went downstairs. Each step felt like an eternity as she took a step down and listened. It became very quiet and still. When she finally reached the bottom of the stairs she quietly called out for her son again but once again responded in silence.

She goes into the kitchen and sees the table flipped over and the chairs broken. The cabinet doors were open and one was hanging almost completely off its hinges. Glass was shattered all on the ground making every step difficult for Anglea.

When she calls out for Raymond a third time, she is cut off by Eddie who is hollering at the top of his lungs. She spun around quickly and dashed towards the stairs. Not knowing she had cut her foot from a shard of glass that was on the ground she slipped and fell on the left side of her hip. Eddie was still crying out in pain pleading for what was happening to him to stop. Anglea got back up to her feet and ran into the bedroom.

"NO!" Anglea shouted, cupped her mouth, and fell to her knees.

Raymond was at the feet of the bed, holding a long knife and stabbing Eddie's foot. His other foot to Anglea looked to be missing three toes. Raymond worked his way up to his knee stabbing and puncturing Eddie's flesh. When he finally reached the top of Eddie's head, Raymond stabbed the right side cheek.

"Please! Angela, stop! You're killing me!" Eddie proclaimed as he spat out blood and saliva.

Anglea is terrified and now bewildered about why Eddie called Raymond her name. When she got to her feet Raymond had taken the knife one last time and slit open Eddie's throat.

The sound then became obsolete as Angela screamed. Raymond cocked his head to the right and smiled at Angela. He puts his feet over the edge of the bed and slides down on his stomach, as Eddie tries to gasp for air but is only choking on his blood. Raymond walks over to Anglea and grabs her by her pinky. She could feel his hands still wet from Eddie's blood but she was stunned and watching her husband die.

"Now," Raymond said. "We can be a family."

The bed that Eddie lay in before taking his last breath was consumed in flames. The fire came from Eddie and began to spread throughout the room, scorching everything and now making its way towards Angela and Raymond. When she tried to run out she learned that her body had become immobilized. She looks down at her feet and tries to move them but they are glued to the floor. Even her arms couldn't move. She tried to shake her body but there was no luck as the fire grew closer and closer to the mother and son.

"Mama" Raymond said, now fully engulfed in flames. "Don't you love me?"

The fire began to kiss Angela's toes and the sound finally came back into the world as she could finally hear herself screaming again.

***

She wakes in a bed screaming and finally having her body properly functioning and moving, she learns that she still is having trouble moving. She was strapped to a bed and was in a dark room. She lets out another scream and that's when a tall doctor with a thick scruffy beard walks in and flips on the lights. Two nurses followed behind him, one nurse who was a female with brown hair had a vaccine shot in one hand and the other nurse who was a male redhead was holding a clipboard with a stack of papers clipped to it.

"Ah," The doctor said, brushing his beard. "You're finally awake again, hmm? And to whom am I speaking today?"

The doctor took the stack of papers away from the red-headed nurse and began flipping through them. Anglea is still in the process of trying to figure out many things at once. The confused and terrifying feeling was still lingering. She looked around in the room which was just four blank walls, a door, and the bed she lay in. Her outfit was a plain white gown that stretched to her feet.

MY FEET! She screamed in her head. Upon examination, she was expecting to find her feet scorched from the flames, but they were fine - clean even. More and more questions were adding up in her brain which was beginning to bang like a loud hard rock drummer who had a thirty-minute solo.

"Where am I?" Angela finally asked. "Where am I, where's my baby? And why the FUCK am I strapped to this bed."

"Baby?" The doctor said, "Ah so we must be talking with Angela, the primary host."

Anglea stared at the doctor with an unamused tension. "Primary host? What the hell is going on someone tell me where my goddamn child is at."

"Anglea listen to me closely." The doctor walked towards her and got to his knees to look directly at her. "You are in the Judy Walls State Hospital for the criminally insane. Mrs. Lewis, you never had a baby."

Anglea could feel her body go limp and cold. She wanted to scream at the doctor that he was lying, but there was something in her that said he was telling the truth.

"That's not true." She whispered. "He killed my husband, I saw it with my own eyes."

The doctor let out a sigh and looked over to the nurse with the needle shot. "Go ahead and show her."

The nurse nodded and she stepped over to the other side of the room exposing a single chair that had a burnt baby doll on it. Anglea was dazed at the plastic toy on the chair and began to laugh.

"What is that supposed to be?" Anglea cackled.

"That Ms. Lewis," The doctor said, "Is Raymond."

She began to laugh even harder as the Doctor stood back up. He took out a ballpoint pen and began to write it down, *Back to square one,* gave the pen a little click, and put it back in his coat pocket.

"I gave birth to an actual baby, not that fake, plastic shit. Now let me get out of this bed!" Angela demanded.

"Ms. Lewis, please understand we're trying our best to help you." The doctor said, handing back the papers and patting the red-headed nurse and he walked out. The brunette nurse - Anglea now seeing name badges on both the nurse and doctor, David Birddy and Megan Nice - takes her place back to where she was standing, blocking out the burnt doll from Angela's view.

I heard their names before, Angela frantically thought, *They're supposed to be dead. Died in a car crash... I heard... their.. names.*

The doctor now bent back down in front of Angela as he stared deeply into her eyes which were heavy and sunken in. "But first I'm going to need you to calm down. We've been through this too many times now. You need to show me some kind of improvement or else more strict consequences will be bestowed on you, Ms. Lewis. May I need to remind you what horrible crimes you committed that wounded yourself up here, hmm?"

Angela was quiet and didn't even move. She stared back at the doctor waiting to see what he had to say.

"Very well then," The doctor continued. "You've been in this fine institution for almost two years now. You and your late husband tried to have kids not once, not twice, but three times. The first child had a miscarriage, and a year later the second child died in a car accident that your husband was involved in. Nearly on the verge of a major breakdown, you and Mr. Lewis attempted to have a third child. Wanting nothing more in life than to have a child, you began to suffer from major depression, personality disorder, and insomnia. When Raymond was born he did not survive his birth and was dead when he was born, due to his umbilical cord choking him to death."

"LIAR!" Angela shouted.

"Ms. Lewis after discovering that you had lost yet another child you went into this state of shock where you didn't speak, eat, or keep up with your basic hygiene. A therapist your husband saw suggested giving you a coping mechanism and Mr. Lewis considered giving you that doll sitting in that chair," He pointed behind Nurse Megan.

"And you cared for it like you would have a normal baby. Four months down the road you began having paranoid thoughts and violent intentions saying that it was the doll that forced you to kill your husband."

Angela could feel her face lose its color and become very cold. "You're lying. Ray-Raymond killed Eddie I didn't-"

"No Angela!" The doctor is now the one who is shouting, "You must leave the fiction world and come back into reality. There was no Raymond, no child was being born, and it was you that stabbed your husband twenty-six times until you slit his throat and set the bed on fire with him still in it. By the time the cops showed up, you were sitting outside of your burning house, holding on to that doll with a devilish grin on your face. You told the cops and investigators that it was the doll who made you do those heinous acts, to which you pleaded insanity in court and wound up here. After a year went by with you in here, you started creating a world where you had a baby and Mr. Lewis and you were a happy family." The doctor squatted two fingers down for 'happy family'.

Angela, not even taking notice, started to cry. In every word, the doctor said she finally saw everything that she did. The child she believed to be caring for and loving was only a doll that her mind perceived to be a real baby. She could see her holding the doll up to her ear as she laughed heartily as if the doll was talking and cracking jokes with her. She could see the fight she got into with Eddie in the kitchen after bringing up the car crash. In hysteria, Anglea began throwing around dinner plates, punching holes in the walls, and trashing the entire kitchen. Later that night after Eddie went to bed, Anglea got out of bed and went into the room where the doll was occupying and picked it up out of the crib that was meant for the real Raymond. She went downstairs picked up the knife and carried it upstairs to end her husband's life. It all started coming back to her consciousness, filling her thoughts with the horrible reality she created.

But she still refused to believe it.

"Ms. Lewis, I need you to show me that you are making progress or else the results may not be in your favor." The doctor said,

Anglea, now feeling enraged, began rocking back and forth trying to loosen the restraints that were holding her down. She began to scream and holler with a bit of white foam coming from her mouth.

"I want my baby!" Angela Pleaded, "You motherfuckers, I want you to take these restraints off me right now and I want to see my baby! Where is my RAYMOND!"

The doctor shook his head in discouragement and clicked his tongue three times. "Such a shame."

He nodded to nurse Megan as she gave him one in return. She began advancing towards Angela flicking the vaccine shot.

"What's that?" Anglea sees the nurse preparing her shot. "You bitch, don't you dare prick me with that. Now bring me my child!"

The nurse pricks Angela in the arm as she gives out one last loud bloody-murder scream. Her body then became relaxed and her mind began to become fuzzy. She could hear the Doctor and the nurse walk out.

"We'll try again in a few months." The doctor said these were the last words Anglea heard before the drug finally sedated her and she fell into a deep sleep.

She dreamt of her and Eddie sitting at the dinner table, putting together a five thousand jigsaw puzzle of a modern

Rome collection. That's when her water broke and she was going into labor.

THE FACE

THEODORE MARKSON LED REPORTER MAXINE RIPLEY down a dark spiral staircase, "It's been locked away you see. Locked away after things got a little crazy."

"You mean after it's killed over thirty people, correct?" Maxine asked. Her hand grazed the cement wall, trying her best not to lose her balance as she traveled down the narrow staircase while holding her tape recorder in the other hand. Of all the days she wanted to wear high heels it just had to be today.

"Sure sure, you could say that," Theodore said, "but many speculate, and this is my assumption as well after having a small glimpse myself, is that the painting has some sort of evil magic behind it."

Maxine scoffs, "Evil magic? Like witchcraft or voodoo?"

"No, no, nothing like that at all. Something... Something far worse than any of that."

Theodore was beginning to pick up the pace a

bit. For an old man, he sure does know how to move. Maxine believes after pulling into the Museum of Religious Artifacts located in Manhattan, New York that Mr. Markson has to be pushing eighty-five years old. His bald head with a cul-de-sac of pearl white hair, his wrinkles that almost seemed to sag off his face, nearly falling off the bone was a dead indicator. When she first arrived he stood outside with his back hunched over that seemed to have straightened just a tad bit as Maxine got out of the car to be greeted by the old geezer. Theodore's hand trembled vigorously as he shook Maxine's hand. He had sort of a limp as he walked as well, perhaps having hip surgery some years back. But now, going down this lengthy spiral staircase, he appears to have a sudden boost of youth-like energy.

"So can you tell me a little bit more about this painting, Mr. Markson?"

Theodore chuckled giving Maxine a cold chill with goosebumps, "Yes I can," he says, "just as long as you don't call me Mr. Markson again. Makes this old fart feel even older."

Maxine agrees to Theodore's request.

"Now, the painter Shelly Mary Naucter was what they used to call the devil in disguise before they announced the evil that is of her paintings. The year was 1904 when she painted The Face of God. The story was she was a schizophrenic and always had these episodes you see. Doctors didn't know what to do about it at the time as pharmaceuticals were not quite the kind that we have today. They would give her something to help her sleep, but she would always have these night terrors that would cause her to wake up with screaming fits.

"She had the most loving and caring parents from what I heard, and they would have done anything to make their daughter better. On the days that were Shelly's 'quiet days' her parents noticed her drawing these very prolific pictures. Outstanded by her performance, her parents would give her lots of paper that you would have thought an entire forest had just lost a bunch of its trees. Shelly would draw and draw, even when her pencil was just an eraser with a sharp point on the other end."

"Then one day, her father got her a collection of blank canvases, which were specifically requested by Shelly herself. She told her parents that she wanted to paint. That she *had* to paint. The look on her face looked to be both passionate and disquieting. But as I said before being the loving parents they were, whatever it took to make their little girl happy they sprang to it immediately and effectively. Shelly would only paint with three colors at that too. Black, red, and gray. Nothing more, nothing less."

Both Maxine and Theodore finally made it to the bottom of the stairwell. Down here it was cold, dank, and something else that Maxine didn't find comforting as well. Like being at the bottom of a cavern that housed something deadly and unforeseen. Theodore took out a ring of keys that were attached to his hip. As he shuffles through the clutter of keys, mumbling something that Maxine couldn't hear, the young news reporter looks up the stairwell. She felt tiny down this hole, having the sensation of what Alice must have felt when she fell down the rabbit hole. A tiny sliver of light came from the top that looked nearly miles away. Theodore made a satisfactory grunt making Maxine jump a little. He found the key, slipping into the keyhole, and to Maxine, it appeared that Theodore had to put all of his strength trying to turn the key. There came a loud clang on the other side when the door finally unlocked that echoed. Theodore swung the door wide open to expose a dark and narrow hallway. A switch was on the wall which Theodore flipped on. One by one the lights came on, showing just how long the hallway truly was. Maxine believed it to be the size of a football field and a half long.

All this for a painting, she thought to herself, shaking her head as she once again immediately regrets wearing high heels.

"Now then," Theodore says, "where was I?"

"Shelly only used Black, red, and gray paints," Maxine said, following right behind Theodore as they walked down the hallway. She began to pick up an odor down here as well.

Her sense of smell, was completely out of whack as she couldn't tell what that smell was. It was something rotten, but also something very sweet as well.

"Ah yes," Theodore continued, "now then when she started to paint, that's when - and pardon my French young lady - shit began to hit the fan. Her first painting she named it *Doggy*. Now I know what you're thinking. You must be envisioning a painting of a German Shepherd or a Golden Retriever, and you would be wrong. Shelly's painting was something like uh… gosh what were those tests where they made you look at blotches of black lines and dots?"

"A Rorschach test?" Maxine answered.

"Yes! Precisely that. You could never tell it was the painting of a dog, but once you stare at it for a very long time, your mind will start to convince you that there was a dog on that canvas. And once you see it, you can't stop seeing it. Once the *Doggy* painting was completed, odd things started to happen. Shelly was still living with her parents at the age of twenty-one, the same year she finished *Doggy*, and one night as Shelly's parents were getting ready for bed when they heard a loud bang come from the front door.

"When her father went to check it out, he walked past Shelly's door and saw her sitting there next to her painting with a devilish smile on her face, looking directly at her father. She didn't speak nor did she move. He went into her room and got down on one knee to ask her what was wrong and if everything was okay. And with that same look on her face, she turns to look at her father and whispers one word, *Doggy*. Puzzled, he got back up to inspect the noise that came from the front door. He peeks out the window before opening it and sees there is no one there. It was a clear night with the moon being the only source of light at the time. He opened the door and began to hear scratches coming from below him. Shelly's father glances down to see a Beagle twitching its legs with its head twisted to one side. The poor bastard must have run full force into the front door and broke its neck."

Maxine winced at this. Not just from the story but from the odor that seemed to be growing much stronger now. She begins to cover her nose as Theodore goes on with his story.

"More and more unusual things start to happen after Shelly begins to do more paintings," Theodore continued, "there was one painting, nothing but red squiggles and nonsense that she dubbed *The Birds*. That next day her parents' entire house had been rained down by tiny cardinals. Another which was called, *Just Hanging Out*, had black and gray lines that if you looked closely, you were able to see a tree with a noose on it. Two days after she completed that one, a boy no older than ten years hung himself on one of the trees in his parent's backyard. Poor fella."

"Now the really painful one was Shelly's painting before she started painting *The Face of God, which* had been an entire canvas filled with red and six lines going down in it. A pattern of three; three black lines and three gray lines. She called this painting, *Mama*. The night after she painted this one Shelly started to scream from her bedroom. When her father went to check on his daughter he ran into her room and she stopped screaming. Shelly was lying in bed sleeping soundly. After walking up to her just to double-check, he began to hear another scream. High and shrilling. And it was coming from his bedroom. When he ran back to inspect the screaming he walked into his room with his wife on fire."

"Jesus Christ," Maxine shutters.

"Ayup, the poor bastard didn't know what to do. He stood there watching his wife burn to a crisp. Until his feet finally got to moving. He grabbed another comforter from his closet to try and snuff out the flames. But as he drew closer he was pushed by some kind of invisible force. Shelly's father went flying out of his bedroom and the door slammed shut. When he tried breaking in, there had been something blocking his way in. Shelly's father was a six-foot-one-inch tall man and weighed at least two hundred and five pounds. Pure muscle he was as he worked as a lumberjack. Yet he couldn't seem to budge the thin wooden door for shit. Pardon my French. The man listened to her scream and scream until it all became quiet. The door finally gave way and when he went in his wife was nothing more than a charred body with smoke rising off the corps."

Theodore and Maxine made it to the end of the hall which had a huge door with many bolts and locks on it. Theodore rummages through his pocket, bringing out a new set of keys.

"So what happened after that?" Maxine said, finding herself intrigued and thinking this might be the story of the year.

Theodore sighs, looking at his keys in his trembling hand with quiet dismay. "At that point, he wanted to kill Shelly. He knew that all of the bad things that were happening around them had some kind of connection with her paintings. He went into her room with an attempt to put a pillow over her face and hold it until she was just as dead as his wife. But… something told him not to. Some sort of power, some kind of voice spoke up to him, telling him that he needed Shelly. He needed her to paint. He watches as Shelly is turned on her back, sleeping the night away. Not even knowing that just down the hall her mother was dead by… something evil.

"So, instead of killing her, he woke her up. Told her to pack her things. He ends up burying his wife just outside his house before they take off in the middle of the night to start a new life as father and daughter. They moved just outside of Manhattan where Shelly's paintings would be sold off five years just after her mother's death. They made millions of dollars. Can you believe that? Off of just some squiggles and lines. Jesus Christ on a stick."

Theodore begins to chuckle a little bit. Maxine watches the old man begin to unlock the huge door upon them, not knowing that her tape recorder which had been at shoulder height, had dropped down to her waist. She shakes her head, raising the recorder back up, "So once they moved close to Manhattan, made a hefty amount of money, what happens then?"

Theodore stops at the last lock. His breathing became long, loud wheezes as he slightly turned his shaking head, giving Maxine a side glance and said with a trembling voice before unlocking the final lock, "Evil happens."

Theodore's throat clicks trying to swallow, turning his head back around to open the door. It swings inward as a new wave of an awful smell that makes Maxine's stomach twist and churn. She reaches into her pocket, bringing out a handkerchief to place over her nose. Maxine takes a step forward and then stops to see Theodore standing there, shaking. She thinks even he is scared to go in there, and he's in charge of this artifact. In a quick moment, Theodore does the sign of the cross with his hand, mumbling some sort of prayer that Maxine couldn't quite understand. Hoping that her recorder can pick up his words for her to listen to later on.

"Are you religious?" Theodore asked, not looking at her but raising his head a little.

"I believe to be spiritual," Maxine says, "in the sense of I believe in a higher power, but not a certain God if that's what you're applying."

Theodore nods his head heavily, "You'll believe in something once we go through here."

His tone. His mannerism. Suddenly it's changed, making Maxine believe the *Pardon my French* of a man has left the building. Leaving her here with someone new. She shakes as a cold chill makes its way down her spine.

Theodore reaches into his pocket one last time and pulls out a small flashlight, turning it on to expose a hallway that makes Maxine believe they are in a sewer. The hall was dark, wet, and somewhat menacing. And was there a sound coming from the other end as well? She listened and could almost make the sound of voices. She begins to have second thoughts about this, just wanting to get a detailed description of Shelly's infamous painting, but something is telling her that she has to see it. That she *needed* to see it. Not just for her job and the story of the lifetime, but for her own reasons herself.

They continued and Theodore returned to his story.

"1904. Ayup, that's the year everything went sideways. Not just for Shelly, but for her father as well. As she painted *The Face of God* she denied anyone to see it. Even her father. He believed that this was just some sort of artist critique he wouldn't understand and he would be just fine with that. As long as she kept the money coming in he wouldn't have to ever see it. The night before she painted The Face of God, her father would walk by her room as he always does before he went to bed just to check on her. That night Shelly would be talking in her sleep. Her father walks in and then stops as he hears her say why she killed his wife. Why she had painted the love of his life to be taken from this world. It was simply because she was afraid. She tossed and turned in her bed as Shelly's father watched the beads of sweat trickle down her forehead. She was afraid because somehow she knew her mother was pregnant. Whatever had possessed her with these abilities to draw such awful things that would later come to fruition would be much stronger than Shelly herself.

THE FACE

And when Shelly's father heard all this he backed away slowly out of his daughter's room. Forgetting everything she had said. As he closes the door Shelly's head turns towards him, still asleep, mind you, and smiles. Shelly's father never mentions that night to her, and he never would.

"It took the young girl six days to paint it. And in those six days, she went through a horrible transformation. She didn't eat, she didn't sleep, she kept a bucket near her so she could piss and shit right in that room. For days the entire house they occupied started to smell like a dirty petting zoo. But Shelly's father didn't mind one bit.

"It was three o'clock in the morning. Right on the dot if I'm not mistaken, when Shelly walked into her father's bedroom. He slept with multiple women, most of them prostitutes. That night he had two women in his bed when one of them let out a scream when they saw Shelly standing there at the doorway like a mannequin holding a paintbrush. She had a vicious grin and was laughing softly to herself. When her father woke up he told the women to leave the house immediately. The prostitutes didn't even have time to grab their clothes. They just ran out in the middle of the night, bare ass and all."

He's not even saying to Pardon his French anymore, Maxine ponders to herself and continues to listen.

"Before her father could even ask what was wrong, he already knew. He could see it in her face. Her painting was complete. When he asked to see it Shelly's smile quickly vanished. She tells him 'No papa, you are forbidden to see it.' He asks her why and the only thing she tells him is that she loves him. Nothing more, nothing less.

"Now Shelly was supposed to be the one to present her painting at the auction in New York City, just as she has always done with her previous works, on August 4th, 1904.

63

But her transformation left her disfigured. Sort of hard to look at is what the head of the painters association, Jonathan Larkus, had told her. And from what I was told, she didn't mind one bit. She even gave him a smile that had exposed most of her teeth either chipped, missing, or black as this hallway we are walking down."

"Now then, this is what you wanted to hear this whole time. The reason why you even showed up to this god-forsaken place. Twenty-nine people attended the auction for Shelly Naucter's brand new painting. The people in attendance were ecstatic as they always were when they were ready to spend tons and tons of money for a whacked out painting. Rich people tend to do this sort of act with their money and why they do it is beyond me. So after two paintings were bidded off for and taken away, the real horrors were actually about to begin. They wheeled in Shelly's painting with a large drape over it. Jonathan Larkus announced the newest addition to Shelly's collection, revealing the name Shelly had given it: The Face of God. They remove the drape off the painting, then something peculiar happens. Usually, once the painting is revealed Larkus would start the bidding and that was that. But instead, silence fell over the auditorium. Everyone in the audience, including Larkus, just seemed to stare directly at the painting. Whether being mesmerized or hypnotized, no one really knows."

"Because everyone that was in attendance died that day?" Maxine said.

"Ayup," Theodore nodded. "One woman stood up, followed by the man right next to her. Then like clockwork, everyone started getting to their feet. Not taking their eyes off the painting in front of them. Then... the screaming begins. The first woman who stood up started screaming as loud as she ever had in her life. She was an older woman, perhaps, oh, in her sixties give or take. And by god did she scream loud enough that she ruptured her vocal cords, and continued to scream afterward. Then for no moral reason at all for what she does, the woman started to peel away her skin. Starting from the wrist then working her way up the arm and finally to her neck. Actually what killed the old biddy is that she tore out her damn jugular."

"What the fuck," Maxine whispered to herself.

"Everyone in attendance had some kind of vile way of killing themselves. Some were the same but many of them suffered and probably had no idea why they were doing what they were doing. Some yanked out their eyes with their bare hands, and many of them beat themselves with their fists until the skulls in their heads cracked and punctured their brains. Others such as Jonathan Larkus took the closest sharp object and slit their throats. The laws would say the cuts damn near decapitated their head right off their necks. By the end it was just one bloody mess and when the laws showed up they didn't know what to call it. After a while, they blamed it on MPI which stands for mass psychogenic illness or in other words mass hysteria. And it wasn't until then that one cop, I forget his name, went to try and retrieve Shelly's painting. When he approached the stage he took one look at the painting, he stopped right where he was at. Paralyzed. Another cop took notice of his partner standing right in front of the painting and saw a small puddle starting to form over his feet. The poor bastard pissed himself. Then without any hesitation, he pulls out his gun and shoots himself right under his chin.

For some reason, the other cop who watched his partner blow his brains out understood something about what was happening. And it had to do something with that painting. When he went to his dead partner on the stage he didn't even glance at the painting. He later told the chief of police that when he stood on that stage there was a different temperature the more he got closer to the painting. Right smack dab in the middle of the stage, it felt cold enough to see your breath. He demanded the painting to be burned and the painter to be brought in for questioning.

"The chief agreed for the painting to be discarded and destroyed immediately but when they arrived back at the auditorium to retrieve the painting it was gone. As they went to see Shelly and her father at their home, they too were long gone. Nothing was left in the house, not even a thumbtack. Empty as if the damn house had just been built."

Finally, Maxine and Theodore arrived at the end of the hallway. A foul odor mixed with the uncomfortable coldness shook Maxine. Her teeth clattered as she went to hold herself in her arms. The recorder in her hand jived up and down. She watches Theodore take out a long single key as they stand right in front of the giant vault-like door. She also took notice that Theodore almost seemed to not mind the coldness, thinking he must be used to it for having to work here for so long. Yet there was something wrong as Maxine stood behind Theodore. She could hear the old man starting to giggle a little bit.

"For nearly three decades the painting had been lost. Until Logan Wallace, a preacher from Long Island found the painting. And not just that, but Shelly as well. Her body looked as if it was decaying and her hair had fallen out in huge clumps. Her arms and legs wrapped around the painting like some kind of anaconda. Mr. Wallace found Shelly lying in a boat that drifted towards shore, and she was laughing. Laughing like a person with no sense left in that sick brain of hers. Mr. Wallace knew the story about The Face of God, on how it was the sole reason for all the deaths in 1904. So he takes Shelly to a mental institute where she spent fifty-two years there. The painting was later brought here where it would be locked away like an inmate in Rikers Island.

"For thirty-eight years Shelly had been pronounced missing as she had simply vanished from the mental institute back in 1984. And as you must know she had a reason for going missing."

Theodore unlocks the vault door as it makes a loud clanging sound, echoing throughout the hallway, making Maxine jump. She drops the recorder from her cold hands and doesn't seem to notice. She watches as the door swings into what would be the last room she would ever enter. Her mouth drops as she sees bones lying all over the floor. The room was ranked with death and vile evil. A large pillar stretched high into the air Maxine never noticed Theodore had been guiding her into the room, crunching on the bones that lay beneath their feet and one getting caught on one of the high heels on Maxine's foot. Her whole body convulses before it goes into a state of shock as she stares high up at the large pillar.

"She had gone missing," Theodore continued, "because The Face of God is what keeps us alive."

Maxine looks somberly over to Theodore. A twisted smile was planted on his face. Theodore grabs the side of Maxine's face, turning it up towards the top of the pillar as she sees a lady who looks nearly hundreds of years old sitting at the edge of the pillar, legs crossed, hands on top of her knees, shrilly cackling as she rocked back and forth. Wearing a long black and silver dress that matched the Snow White of her hair. Her head twirled and spun madly as she sat right in front of the Face of God.

"My daughter must feed her painting. And we thank you for your contribution."

Maxine looked directly at the painting and felt her whole body go warm and numb. Her bladder began to release itself as it trickled down her legs. She blinks furiously as tears begin to flood her cheeks. Theodore lets go of her face, walks out of the room, and sees the tape recorder lying on the ground. He kicked the recorder into the room and landed next to a pile of bones. Theodore goes back in to crush the recorder with his foot, then walks out with a hideous wheezing laughter, closing the door behind him.

Maxine screams until she is unable to scream anymore as she begins to peel off the skin on her wrists.

ELIZA

CHILDREN CAN BE PECULIAR AT TIMES. A bit strange. A bit weird. Never seeming to not be hungry. For Eliza, all three can be described perfectly for this young boy, who would soon be kidnapped by a couple of sex traffickers. But before Eliza had been snatched off the corner of the sidewalk by two large and round sex trafficking men, he was watching as the puffy white clouds whisked on by, not having a care in the world.

The nine-year-old boy was not waiting for anything in particular, he had been enjoying his day. His stomach made a loud rumble, notifying him that he should eat something and soon. As he looked down the road no other cars were passing by. At the end of the block had been an older Hispanic man, with a thick graying mustache and round glasses mowing his lawn. The boy smiled at the man, watching him stop his mower to wipe the sweat off his forehead, walking over to his porch to take a sip of freshly squeezed lemonade his wife brought out to him earlier. While watching the man his stomach let out another rumble.

The man looked over to the boy, getting a queer sensation. The boy with long shaggy brown hair, and dark green eyes that could even be seen just a few yards away he stood, had been staring at him with a smile that looked innocent, but also… blank. He wore what appeared to be a thick maroon cotton sweater with some sort of logo on the front. To the man, it looked to be a cross or a bold lowercase T. The Hispanic man got more hot and heated just by looking at him. He thought, *man, that boy is gonna have a heat stroke in this weather wearing that sweater. And in jeans too, chinga wey!* And it had been a very hot day. It's been hot for the past few weeks the entire month of July, but today just seemed excruciating. The man nodded towards the boy in a sort of hello gesture, giving a soft crooked smile his way. Eliza just kept staring at him, almost as if he had been stuck in time. Raising his eyebrows, the man took another sip of his lemonade before returning to tending to his lawn.

Eliza licked his lips and started towards the man, then stopped as he watched a white van with no windows turn down the block, strolling towards his way. The young boy watched as the van's side door began to slide open. A huge man with tattoos all over his arms, neck, and one on his face gave the boy a venomous smile before he stepped out of the van, picked up the boy by his waist, and jumped back into the van with Eliza in his arms. The van started to pick up speed once more and drove around the corner. The Hispanic man never saw this little ordeal take place as his back was facing them as he was pushing his lawnmower. When he turned he noticed the little boy was not standing there anymore, feeling a strange sense of relief and panic all at once.

Eliza had been placed on the ground in the back of the van as his hands were being bound together by duct tape along with his knees and finally his ankles. Checking his pockets the man only finds a small school identification card. On it was the boy with a smile showing off his pearly whites. The name on the card read Eliza A. Ocampo and he attended Sul Ross Elementary the past year. The man puts the card into his pocket and continues to secure more duct tape. As this was all being done Eliza never once took his eyes off the man's face, particularly looking at the man's face tattoo which happened to be three numbers: 731. The man with the face tattoo looked at the little boy, feeling a cold chill run across his body as the boy had been staring at him, not saying a word with a smile that pushed his cheeks high enough to expose the small dimples on the side of his mouth. The man's left eye twitched for a bit, backing away as he didn't take his eyes off Eliza returning to the front passenger seat with Eliza never taking his eyes off the man.

"That's one down and four more to go," the driver said. He studied his partner's face and saw a bit of concern. "What the fuck is wrong with you, Roger?"

"That's one creepy kid," the man known as Roger said.

The driver looked back through his rearview mirror and saw the boy looking directly at him through the mirror, smiling. "Yeah, I see what you mean, who the fuck wears a sweater in this kind of heat?"

"Nah," Roger said, keeping an eye out for any other potential kids to steal, "is he still looking up here, Sergio?"

"Yeah, so what," Sergio snickers. "Probably about to piss his pants because he's so scared. Maybe smiling is his way of crying. You know how fucking weird kids can be these days." Sergio takes another look at Eliza who had still been staring at him. He thinks, *Has this kid even blinked?*

Eliza's stomach begins to rumble once more.

After an hour that goes by, Eliza has fallen asleep. Sergio looks through the rearview mirror, feeling satisfaction with the boy falling asleep and actually, not putting up much of a fight, and not having to tell a whining brat to shut the fuck up as he usually has to. This kid was odd, yes, but he was making his job much easier. Roger pointed out a couple of kids playing basketball on a run-down court. Sergio smiled, having a gold canine tooth glimmer viciously. He drove down the block, busting a U-turn, then finding a good parking spot to wait for the perfect opportunity to strike. Just as they did with Eliza. Not drawing any attention as the side of the van looked like a normal working truck with the words, *Ricardo's Internet Service* plastered on each side with indigo lettering. Always parking near a telephone pole to blend in with the area.

Thirty minutes passed as the two men watched two girls who looked like they were twins about nine or ten years old and a small white boy who was perhaps a few years younger. Perhaps the same age as Eliza who was still sleeping away. Or at least that's what he wanted the two men to believe as one eye popped open wide, watching the two men with a certain interest. The three kids stopped playing their basketball game. Laughing loud enough that sounded like money to Roger and Sergio's ears. Sergio looked up into the rearview mirror, seeing that Eliza had still been asleep. As he looked back towards the kids outside he watched them as they were unfortunate enough to be walking towards their van.

The coast was clear. There was no one watching these kids except for what evil lurks inside Ricardo's Internet Servicing van. "Get ready," Sergio instructed. He took one last look into the rearview mirror and suddenly felt cold. Eliza had been sitting upright, looking directly at him through the mirror with that dastardly smile back on his face. Sergio's lip curls, thinking, *If this kid fucks it up and makes some kind of scene we're screwed. Dammit Roger, why didn't you tape that kid's mouth shut?! That way I won't have to look at his stupid grin.*

Eliza chuckled. As if he had read Sergio's thoughts.

Roger got into the back of the van, putting his hand on the door waiting to snatch the kids into the van. Sergio followed right behind him, putting a small gun into the back of his pants and then covering it with the tail of his shirt.

"Listen to me kid," Sergio said looking directly at Eliza, "if you make any kind of sound, I will kill you. Got it?"

Eliza's smile starts to fade. His eyes became narrow, almost stoned-like. He turns his head away from the door, not saying anything in return. Sergio nods his head, thinking that the kid understands. Also pondering if the kid is some sort of mute. Either way, he wasn't going to kill the kid, that would be like throwing your money into a blender to make a cash smoothie out of it. Sergio looks at Roger, giving a nod which means it was go time.

Roger cracks the side of the door just a tad, letting the outside world into the van to hear the three kids approaching as they were still laughing and talking amongst each other. Roger sees one of the kids passing the front of the van, he counts two Mississippi's then opens the van door in a quick haste. The three kids stood in front of them, dumbstruck and startled. Roger hopped out of the van and took the two little girls by their waist as they started to put up a fight. Sergio leaped after the boy as he started to run, only to not get far as he tripped over his feet. Sergio grabbed the ninety-eight-pound boy by the top of his pants, throwing him to the van and taking his gun from behind him. He points the gun at all three newcomers to the van, telling the scared, crying, yelling kids to shut the fuck up!

Roger slams the door shut behind them after putting the girls inside the van. He checks his cheek on the same side the tattoo was on, seeing that one of the girls had clawed him good enough to draw blood. He wipes away what he can as he gets the duct tape ready, listening to the three kids beg and plead for their lives.

"Shut the fuck up or else I'm going to put a goddamn bullet into your skulls!" Sergio yelled.

All three kids went quiet. Eliza still had his head facing the other way, not paying any attention to what was happening a few inches away from him. He listened to the sound of the rip of the tape coming off the roll then the quick snap of it coming off. studying the sound of just how brittle the tape was as he started to wiggle his wrists. As he did he started to pull his wrists apart, feeling the duct tape stretch far enough that it was beginning to loosen. His sly little smile had come back on his face.

After Roger was finished securing the children both men got back up to the front of the van. Checking the area once more to see if anyone had been watching, but the area was still empty. Roger and Sergio bumped fists as the van started up and drove away.

"One more baby!" Roger said, rapping his hands on the dashboard in a happy tone, "Boss man is going to pay us well for delivering these kids days early! Let me find out you have a four-leaf clover hidden in your back pocket!"

As the the two men in the front seat cheered and raved, the four kids sat in the back looking from one to another. The three kids whimpered, thinking horrible thoughts of what could happen to them. One of the black girls that had two puffy pom poms of hair on each side opened her mouth to ask the two men what they had planned for them, then closed her mouth as she remembered what the man with the gun had told them if they had said a word. The little white boy who had an American flag on his white t-shirt with a red Old Navy logo at the top scooted his way toward Eliza. Eliza watched the boy with gleeful curiosity, feeling the duct tape on his wrists grow much looser.

"I'm scared," Old Navy boy had said, "I want my daddy."

"Shh," The girl with the afro pom poms hissed. She looked up towards the two men in the front seats who seemed to have not noticed them, not yet at least. The back of the van was big enough to put at least two dozen more kids back there and still have plenty of legroom. It reeked in the van. The smell of what the two black girl's auntie called her special smoke, which in all was just marijuana, lingered thickly and unpleasantly. On one side the girl noticed a bunch of cables and wires. Below that had been what appeared to be a work bag. She thought maybe there might be something in there to cut the duct tape with. As she scanned the rest of the van her eyes ran across Eliza's. She shuddered as he looked at him watching her with a great big smile, licking his lips. His eyes, mouth, and entire aurora reminded her of a story her mother read her and her sister when they were younger called Red Riding Hood. And this little boy who was staring at her was the big bad wolf.

But he's just a kid, The little black girl thought, *just a kid, like us. He can't be as dangerous as the two fat men... Can he?*

"What's your name?" The girl asked.

Eliza looked at her with a smile that just gave her the creeps. The little boy who sat next to Eliza was now becoming worried about Eliza as well. There was a look in his eyes that didn't seem right, didn't feel right. No sir-y Bob.

"Kid what's your name," The girl whispered a little louder.

Eliza's smile grew into a dim expression. A new look of worry ran across his face and quickly whipped his head towards the two men in the front seats as he heard Sergio let out a long sigh.

"I thought I told you kids to shut the fuck up!" Sergio bellowed. "Who wants to die first, hmm? Speak now and I'll forever end your peace!"

None of the kids said a word. The Old Navy boy started to inch away from Eliza. Not sure which one would be worse to sit next to Eliza or the two men? But that question was ludicrous of course. The two men would be much worse. The kid was also bound together just as he and his two best friends were. So why does he feel so scared around Eliza? The Old Navy boy looked over to Eliza once more. Eliza's gaze was looking sharply at the two men. The gears were turning in the kid's head from where the Old Navy boy had been sitting, having a feeling it was not a good one. The Old Navy boy glanced down at the boy's wrist, feeling much more paranoid now as he watched Eliza begin to pull apart his duct tape. How? How is he doing that? The Old Navy boy struggled to move his wrists but was nowhere nearly as successful as the boy sitting right next to him. Suddenly, like a fresh wave on the beach hitting you at the hottest time of the day, the Old Navy boy started to feel relieved. Perhaps this boy would become their savior. It is a little outlandish to think that there are such things as superheroes, but what if today would be the day that there were superheroes, and this boy was one of them? Like a mini Superman or Captain America.

The Old Navy boy looked back up from Eliza's wrists as they had stopped moving only to find that he locked eyes with Eliza's. And he was smiling right at him. The Old Navy boy tried to offer a smile back at him, but a new wave of fear washed over him. Because if there are such things as superheroes then that can only mean there are such things as villains. So which one did that make the boy with the ominous smile?

Friend or Foe?

The ride in the van was a quiet one, only to get much worse in the next few hours.

After driving for nearly two hours, the day was now beginning to slip away into dusk. The clouds were now a dark pink with the sky a light orange and blue. The two girls and the Old Navy Boy pass out asleep in the back, Eliza not taking his eyes off the two men in the front seats, and Sergio begins to curse in Spanish. The van was going to need gas pretty soon. They were not as fortunate at finding their last kid as they had been with the previous four that sat in the back of the van. Roger looked over to Sergio, with a joint in his hand as he started to cough.

Roger cleared his throat, "What," he coughed some more. Finally catching his breath he continued, "What's wrong?"

"I'm gonna have to fill up soon, probably gonna have to feed the little brats as well."

Eliza's eyes grew wide at this. He became so excited that he finally found the strength to rip the duct tape that bound his wrists off of him. He felt his time to feed would be soon enough, taking a look at the three sleeping children in the back seat.

"Good, because I'm getting hungry as fuck too," Roger said, "I also got to piss like a mother fucker. Been holding it for the past hour."

"Well speak up next time vato," Sergio snickered. "Could have let you piss while I fill up the van."

"Look," Roger pointed to his left, "There's a Shell station right there. Bitch looks empty enough. Pull over."

Sergio checked his side mirrors and then into his rearview mirror to check on the kids. The three new ones were still asleep, hunched over each other like a family of foxes. Then as he looked at Eliza, his lip began to curl as the little boy now had an even bigger smile on his face. Exposing his teeth that looked to be sharp, sort of like tiny shark teeth. Sergio started to feel angry, not knowing why. Perhaps this kid knows something he doesn't and that just didn't sit right with him.

"What the *fuck* are you smiling at cabrón?" Sergio raged. It was loud enough that he had startled the three other kids awake. Eliza's smile goes back down. Not showing his teeth but still looking directly at Sergio through the mirror.

"What happened?" Roger queried.

"That pinche tu madre keeps looking at me. I can't wait to get rid of that one." Sergio started to pull into the gas station. Picking the furthest pump from the store, putting the van into park, then picking up his gun that sat in the side of the door and holding it to the side of his head. Both men turned to look at the kids with a fowl expression on their faces.

"Alright, listen up and listen carefully," Sergio started to say, looking at the frightened looks on the two girls and the Old Navy boy's faces, not paying any attention to Eliza. "We're going to go into this store. If any of you try any dumb shit," Sergio cocks his gun and points it at the kids in the back, "I will unload every bullet in this gun on you. Don't yell, don't try to draw any attention, and don't even think of escaping. As if you can." Sergio smiled madly and started to cackle. Roger chuckled himself as both men got out of the van, making their way into the store and leaving the kids in the van.

The girl with the pom pom afro saw this as an opportunity to try to look for anything that could help them escape. She crawled her way like a worm over to the work bag she had been eyeing this whole time. Her sister and the Old Navy boy watched with quiet fascination. When she reached the bag her luck was on her side, seeing that the bag was wide open. But when she looked into the bag all of her luck had gone cold. The bag was empty. Perhaps some sort of decoy if the fat evil men were to be pulled over by the cops.

"Drats!" The girl said. Hawking a mean loogie and spitting it into the bag. "We gotta think of something to get out of here."

The Old Navy Boy looked at his friend with silent horror. What could they do? They were trapped like rats. He searched everywhere around the van to help cut the duct tape off of their wrists. The three all searched not coming up with anything at all. Suddenly they began to hear the sound of something rumbling. It was loud as the three children all turned their heads towards the noise. They all looked at Eliza as his head was hung low, down to his chin. His chest heaved in and out so rapidly that it appeared that he was having some sort of seizure. Eliza's hair covered most of his face to mask the grin of a madman. The grin of someone with a terrible secret.

The grin of someone hungry.

Eliza lifted his arms to expose that his tape was split in two, his wrists and arms were free from their bounds. With no trouble at all, he tears off the tape that held together his legs and ankles. Planting his feet wide apart he stood up, not using his hands as his whole body propped upwards, head still hung low. There came a new sound of something snapping like thick branches coming off a tree. His neck twitches to one side of his shoulder then over to the next side. His fingers were bulging in and out of his hand. The children listened as his breath started to become violent with wheezes. Then his whole body went still. Paused in that moment in time the three children watched in horror as a new evil was upon them. They watched as Eliza began to turn his back on them, removing the thick sweater from him. Once his back was completely exposed the children screamed. They screamed for someone to help them, but there was no one outside of the van to hear. The children who were tied up, once thinking of ways of escaping were now being torn to shreds and devoured by Eliza. Blood and skin being tossed around the back of the van as their screams ran on.

From the outside, the van began to rock from side to side. The children's screams were muffled along with a terrible sounds of ripping, tearing, and a hiss that almost resembled the hiss of an alligator before it all went quiet along with the van coming to a standstill. The two men inside never noticed the van rocking back and forth and losing three children in the process.

Now call it out of luck, or bad timing if you will, at the time the van had stopped rocking back and forth just outside of the gas station, a police cruiser came rolling in, parking just outside of the store. Lieutenant Blakey, a tall, muscular, bald black man steps out of his cruiser, beginning to start his night shift right just as he has always been doing for the past thirteen years now of getting his cup of coffee and buying his wife her usual lottery scratch-offs. *Someday*, Mrs. Blakey tells her husband every once in a blue moon, *I'm going to win it big for the both of us. That way we won't have to worry about ever having to go to work, and I won't have to constantly worry about you not coming back home.* Sure. Whatever you say dear. Got to keep the missus happy with her wishful thoughts. A happy wife is a happy -

He enters the station and notices one of the men in the far corner looking at the beers and malt liquors. He matches a description of one of the kidnappers that had been spotted a few weeks ago. He looks back outside. As he did the lights above the gas pumps came on like a man with a brilliant idea. He sees a white van with the same description as the witness claims to see a small child whisked away. Roger turns his head once more looking up to grab a Modelo from the top shelf. Lieutenant Blakey is now certain that the man in the far corner is the kidnapper. Roger closes the door, having Blakey walk down the aisle he is in, head hung close to his walkie. Quietly asking for immediate backup and giving his location. Roger walked up to the counter, telling the clerk about putting fifty dollars for the pump with the van next to it.

"And which pump would that one be sir?" The clerk asked him.

"I just said the one with the van out there!" Roger insisted. He peaks over outside, "It's pump number -"

Roger's eyes grew wide and his heart started to palpitate. He stares directly at the cop car that was parked right outside in front of the station door. He felt a cold chill wash over him and before he could even turn around, Roger heard the sound of a gun being cocked right behind him.

"Don't move," Lieutenant Blakey instructed. "Roger Fumer, you are under arrest for kidnapping and child sex trafficking."

Roger slowly begins to put his hands up. He utters a little chuckle under his breath, looking directly at the clerk in front of him, whose face is bright red and shaking like a scared puppy. "Roger who? Nah, man, I think you have the wrong guy." He said coolly.

"I know exactly who you are," Blakey said, stepping up to Roger. His gun was mere inches away from the back of Roger's head. Ready to pull the trigger if he felt any intimate danger being presented by the man in front of him. "I've seen your face, and not many people have that stupid face tattoo such as the one as yours. Now put your hands behind your back and get on your knees."

"Officer I assure you-"

"That's *Lieutenant*, you mother fucker!" Blakey now has his gun almost pressing against the back of Roger's head. *I should shoot him right now.* Blakey pondered, *shoot him right now! No one will miss him. I can say that he came on to me. Convince the cashier to get rid of the surveillance footage if I offered him enough money.* "I said on your knees god dammit!"

Roger chuckled again, "Nah, I don't think so."

Blakey pressed his gun against Roger's head. "I'm warning you! I'm not going to-"

A loud *BANG* shot off into the gas station. The clerk behind the counter uttered a high squeal of a scream. Blood splattered all over the back of Roger's head. Roger turned quickly enough to see the side of the lieutenant's head was shot from one side to the other. Brain matter was all over the floor and some on the side of Roger's hair. He looks to see smoke coming out the barrel of the gun Sergio was holding. The lieutenant fell to the floor with a hard thud.

Roger looked over to Sergio, lip curling in disgust and anger, "What the *fuck* man!"

"A thank you would be nice!" Sergio cocked the gun again, "Come on we got to go! We can fill up at another gas station. We got to get out of here before more of them show up. Go get the van started!"

"What are you finna do?"

"Get rid of the footage and the witness too?"

The clerk backed to the wall of cigarettes behind him. A bunch of Marlboros, Camels, and Pall Malls came tumbling down in front of him, "No please don't." The clerk whimpered. "I won't say a word. I promise! Don't kill me!"

Roger nodded his head, he took off outside and could already hear the warble of cop cars closing in on them.

"Hurry up!" Roger shouted inside. "I hear them coming already!"

Sergio gave him a nod in return and watched Roger take off to the van. "Sorry kid, but I don't work on promises."

"No! Please! Don't!"

Sergio fires the gun two times. The bullets hit the clerk both times, one in the shoulder and one in the head. The clerk slumps down onto the ground as a pool of blood starts to flood the floor below him.

Outside, Roger quickly hops into the van and cranks it up. He puts the van into drive, pulling it around to the front of the store to wait on his partner. The warble of sirens was drawing closer. Roger looks towards the sound of sirens and can see the bright red and blue lights illuminating the darkness down the road. He sees Sergio now running out from the back of the store towards the front. Roger hops over to the passenger side, opens the glove compartment, takes out a sawed-off shotgun, and loads up the gun as Sergio hops into the driver's seat.

"Hold on," Sergio yells, "it's about to get bumpy!"

Sergio steps on the gas. The tires below let out a loud screech as the van took off as they fled from the scene of the unexpected crime not to mention the on pursuit cops. Roger looks out the side mirror, seeing the cop cars growing ever so close to them.

"Faster," Roger proclaims, "faster! They're gaining on us."

"Just have your gun ready! I'm gonna try to get them to go to your side."

Roger watches as he sees three cop cars now following their tail. Sergio pulls the van to the other side of the road. The first cop car comes from behind and rams the back end of the van, having Sergio and Roger jump forward a bit. Sergio curses in Spanish. The cop car is now driving towards the passenger side. Roger begins to roll down his window. Watching for the perfect opportunity to take his shot. The two other cop cars are now moving towards the back of the van fixing to also ram into it. Roger could see his opportunity as the cop car was now in the middle of the van. He pokes half of his body out, the gun on his shoulder, one eye closed, pumping the shotgun and fires it at the driver and sees blood splatter all over the windshield of the car. The car swerves first to the left, losing the speed it once had as it began to now veer to the right. It hits one of the cars behind the van, causing a domino effect to the car right next to it as both cars turn to their sides and drive off into a ditch on the side of the road. The car with the now dead cop crashes into the back of another cop car, trapping it in place of the ditch. Sergio and Roger watch in their side view mirror as the cop cars start to become tiny little specks and flashing lights until they are not seen anymore.

"Holy shit," Sergio raved, "Mother fucking John Wick in the house!"

"God damn that was too close." Roger let out a sigh of relief.

"Woo hoo *hoo!* Can't nobody fuck with us!"

"We still need to get gas and probably can't stop for a while now."

"Aye don't worry, we just need to Jack us another ride like this one vato. I'm still waiting for that thank you for saving your ass back there."

Roger looked at Sergio with bewilderment, "Saving my ass? Bitch I had it all under control before you came in like Clint Fucking Eastwood."

"Clint Eastwood huh," Sergio cackled loudly. "I like that! I'll take that as my thanks!"

Sergio watches the road and sees a sign reading the next few towns that are coming up. Closes one being in the next twelve miles. He looks down at the gas gauge, suspecting that they should be good if not pushing it. He looks up to see another sign that reads, *bridge barrier down, drive cautiously.* Sergio watched his side mirror to see if any more cops were coming after them, yet the coast was all clear. Not even the sound of a cop car could be heard. He notices that nothing can be heard except the sound of both men breathing extremely heavily. Both were heavy set men and after Sergio ran from the back of the store to the van and then tried to outrun the cops he felt almost like an asthma patient. Still, it did seem eerily quiet.

"Check on the kids will ya," Sergio said, taking out another joint from a cigarette box in the cup holder. "They seem awfully quiet for all the shit we went through."

Roger turns in his seat. His eyes scanned every inch of the darkened back of the van and was flabbergasted. "What the fuck!" He draws closer towards the back still in his seat and yet he doesn't see one sign of any kids in the back seat. Roger gets to his feet, telling Sergio to hit the lights for the back of the van. Sergio toggles the switch above him, having the lights show the horrors of the back of the van.

The entire back was consumed in a mass amount of blood. The floor, the roof, and the sides of the van are a complete mess of wet crimson red. Roger shutters as he steps deeply towards the back, ready to puke everywhere. He looks down and sees a tattered shirt that appears to be ripped to pieces. Picking it up which dripped with a thick coat of blood, he can see that the shirt had part of the American flag on it. Above only read, *Ol* and *Nav.*

"Sergio, what the fuck happened in here?" Roger said still holding the shirt in his hand.

As Roger turned around he could feel his heart racing faster. He holds his breath, torn from being confused, enraged, and now most of all terrified. He sees Eliza standing right behind Sergio's seat. He is staring up at Roger, mouth dripping with wet blood, smiling wanly up at him. Exposing sharp jagged teeth that were coated in red. Too stunned to move and too confused to say anything Roger watches as Eliza puts his hands on each side of Sergio's head. Sergio screams as his head begins to cave in. Not knowing who or what is going on as he hears his skull begin to crack. Then in a quick instant, Eliza spins Sergio's head completely around. The sound of his neck making a crack reminded the young twisted boy of the duct tape when it was ripped off the roll. The van now picking up speed as Sergio's dead weight causes his foot to lay heavy on the gas pedal. Roger staggers backward. He slips on the fresh wet blood on the floor, landing right on his buttocks, and slides to the back. He watches as Eliza grabs hold of Sergio's neck and begins to pull. Having his head ripped away from his body along with his spine still attached to the bottom of his neck.

"What the fu-" Were the only words Roger was able to speak before the van ran off the road, heading down a steep hill instead of crashing where the barrier for the bridge they were crossing should have been.

The front of the van hits a dead log at a fair amount of speed that sends the nose end upwards. Roger becomes suspended in mid-air before the van comes crashing back down. It rolls six, seven, eight times before it arrives at the bottom of the hill. All four wheels were completely tarnished as the rims were cracked and broken. The side of the van nearly caved in. A small stream of smoke begins to rise from the engine of the van. The windshield was blown off as the van came tumbling down. Sergio's headless body lies outstretched at the front of the van.

Roger, who somehow miraculously survived the crash, crawls his way towards the side door. A tremendous amount of pain sends fiery flares from his legs that make him wince. His head throbbed and there was blood coming from the top of his head from a great big gash above his eyebrow. He reaches for the door handle, half blind as blood begins to pour over his left eye. Finally managing to take hold of the door handle he swings the door open. Letting the night air hit his bruised, battered, and aching body as he crawls out of the van cursing into the air. When he falls out he plants his head into the ground to scream and writhe in pain. Tears begin to spill down his face as he has never felt a vast amount of pain.

This pain, Roger thought to himself, *This pain! I can't stand this pain! Please god, make this pain go away!*

Roger lifts his head. He turns his body over and looks down at his legs. His eyes were shaking. His right ankle was twisted over to the side, almost laying completely flat. His left ankle had bones that had been punctured out of the skin. His legs were bloody and white from the bones coming out of his shins. He reaches to touch them and lets out a cry into the air.

There came a loud knock coming from the van. Roger holds his mouth shut tightly with his hands. The knocks begin to turn into bangs as the van begins to creak and rock from side to side.

BANG...! BANG...... CRASH!

Roger lets out a soft whimper, nearly jumping out of his skin when the driver's side door goes flying off the van with a loud rumble and lands far away. He listens as something crawls out of the van with hard and heavy hooves like a really big deer. His eyes were wet, watching whatever monstrosity was crawling out of the van and now making its way around towards the front. Roger tries again to crawl, but the pain not just in his legs but his entire body restricts him from moving anymore. Before whatever had crawled out of the van made it to the other side with Roger the hoove footsteps suddenly stopped. The cry of a lonely pigeon echoes out from the heavy forest and is the only sound that is heard.

Finally, Eliza's head peers from the other side, twisted as it looked at Roger with a sinister smile. At first, it was the only part of the boy Roger could see. He seemed to be crawling as his head was low to the ground.

Roger cried out with spit and blood flying out of his mouth, "*FUCK YO-*" then watches as something beyond any horrors Roger has ever seen.

Eliza's smile goes away in a blink of an eye. His head begins to snap and twist, having his head face the ground. Then it begins to rise above the hood of the van, stepping out to expose this animal-like body of his. But to Roger, this was not a typical animal he'd ever seen. This boy was not human, nor animal but something far worse than any nightmare Roger has ever dreamed. Long bones were protruding out of Eliza's elbows that were being used to walk on. His head slowly bobbed up and down as if to be saying yes… yes… yes. It was twisted around to where his head was facing the back. Eliza's body seemed to be stretched an extra five feet. His legs were long and skinny which were badly flooded from his jeans. His sweater was no longer on his body. There seemed to be chattering coming from somewhere on the boy that sounded like a typewriter hitting a porcelain wall. God, the sound was becoming unbearable to Roger as the sound seemed to crescendo as this creature grew closer to him. Finally, Eliza was beginning to crawl over Roger, seeing with his own eyes as Eliza's head bobbing up and down over him with that horrible grin on his face, his tiny shark-like teeth covered in blood as it goes right over Roger's head. And now the chattering sound he had been hearing turned out to be over fifty tiny mouths with razor-sharp teeth all over the boy's back, rapidly opening and closing as the teeth mashed together, waiting to be fed. In the center of Eliza's back was a huge mouth slightly open to expose the fangs that were as black as the nighttime sky. The mouth in the center seemed to be smiling as it hovered over Roger, drawing closer as the smell of something wretched and dead was breathing down on him.

"What the fuck are you?" Roger cried out.

"Just a weird kid," the huge mouth spoke in a low demonic voice, "just a weird kid, here to take the pain away."

Eliza's head begins to bob up and down much faster now as he bends his back downwards. The huge monstrous mouth takes a huge bite out of the man's face and rips off the face tattoo before the other tiny mouths begin to feast on Roger's entire body. Leaving no trace of a body to be found when the police that was in pursuit would later discover the van. No bodies, just a huge pile of blood left everywhere around the broken and beaten van.

✳✳✳

A week later as police searched neighboring cities that surrounded the van that could be harboring the suspects, Roger and Sergio, not having any leads, a bus would pull up to its stop on the side of the road letting a large group of people on to get them to their destination. The crowd chattered amongst themselves and some sat by themselves, minding their own business. One of the passengers on board was a little boy with a thick sweater with a large cross in the center and wearing jeans that sat in the back of the bus all alone. He watches the crowd with quiet curiosity as he smiles wide and big. Pushing his cheeks high to expose the deep dimples on the side of his mouth, as his stomach begins to rumble.

UNDERNEATH GRANDPA'S FIELD

I WILL NEVER FORGET THE YEAR I went to my grandfather's farm one summer as a teenager. I was thirteen going on fourteen and it would be the last year I got to spend with my old man. The time my mother would still call me Dezzy when my grandpa would call me by my actual name, Desmond. To the townsfolk of Caldwell, he was known as the colonel as he spent time fighting Nazis and Koreans in his prime time. But to me, he will always be my grandpa Lewis. I will never forget how hot it was that year as well.

My mother worked as a traveling agent who went from the southern states, such as New Mexico, Louisiana, Alabama, and some parts of Florida. By the end of the summer before she would head back to Texas she would end her trip with the other agents in Atlanta. She would leave me with my grandfather who I adored. Grandpa Lewis had land that, to me at least being a child to my adolescent days, seemed like the biggest land I could have ever roamed. He had lots of cows, chickens, a few horses, and a pond that had plenty of ducks and geese that would swim around.

From the end of May through the first week of August, my grandfather would have me help him around the farm and his land. In return, he would pay me a great amount of money and have the most amazing food I could have ever eaten. Grandpa Lewis would show me how to cook some of the foods I liked, chicken and dumplings, steaks, and pork chops were what I learned to make, and even though it didn't come out quite as good as he would make it, it was still very delicious.

But there would be some days when he would be... a total mystery to me. I wouldn't think anything of it because I always thought a lot of older people around my grandfather's age acted quite peculiarly. They had their ways of doing certain things that young folk would not quite understand and at the time I didn't mind one bit. Yet, that last summer I spent with him on his farm in his last years had made me feel a certain way towards him. Very daunting. It's been fifteen years since that day I went to see what Grandpa was hiding under his field and for a while now I always suspected it to be a dream. Until I came across the old photograph that I found that day he went off into town, leaving me behind to play on my Game Boy and watch TV. That old photograph of him and the ghosts that lived underneath his field.

The night before I went exploring something I believe shouldn't have been explored, it was storming mighty heavy. The rain came down in huge drops nearly causing the pond out in the field to overflow and started making its way towards the barn. The thunder made the lights flicker, the TV would sometimes lose signal and there was a certain sound that I couldn't quite make out. A sound that made my grandfather look as if he was having a PTSD fit. It was the sound of an alarm and machinery working. Gears were grinding which reminded me of a train that was coming to a stop. But I knew that sound couldn't be what I thought to be on the count that we lived far away from any type of train tracks. That was more towards the town than it was my grandfather's home.

I remember how quickly Grandpa Lewis got up from his seat that one stormy night because he was a fairly old man who needed to walk with a cane. He walked past the TV which was showing the professional wrestling program we loved to watch and over to the front window in a quick haste. He peered through the window shades to study the barn that was right across from his home. Grandpa made an audible gasp that sounded like he was beginning to choke on his spit. He walked past the TV again, this time nearly skipping and grunting.

"Grandpa," I said, looking at him with wide eyes and my heart beating in my throat. "What's wrong?"

"Oh it's nothing, my boy," Grandpa said as he started to put his raincoat on standing at the front door. "It's nothing, I just have to check on something in the barn.

"Should I come with you?" I said starting to get up.

"*No,*" he nearly hissed at me. Grandpa could see that I was starting to get a little frightened then he flashed me a small smile. "No, no. I'll be fine. The storm is nasty out there and I don't need you to be catching a cold. Your mom would hang me out to dry if I got you to catch a summer cold. Just wait right here. Keep watching TV so you can tell me who beat up who while I was gone. I'll be back in two shakes of a duck's tail."

He opened the door and the wind of the storm came gushing right through. Grandpa started to walk out, turned to look at me, and said, "Promise me you'll stay right here Desmond,"

I was speechless but then I started to think this was one of those old people moments that only grown-ups could handle. The noise of the machinery seemed much louder as the door was open. Even louder than the thunder that boomed after a strong lightning flash. I pressed my lips together and nodded. Grandpa in return gave me a crooked smile, nodding himself, and then he headed off towards the barn.

I ran over to the window to watch as he hobbled down to the barn. I watched as he opened both doors to the barn. Seeing something I've never seen before. There was bright red and white light softly flashing somewhere deep in the barn. He walked in and closed the doors behind him. I started to feel cold. Goosebumps started to spread down my body. Thunder quaked over my head, making me jump. I began to walk back to the couch and watch a little bit of wrestling. On it, Stone Cold Steve Austin was cursing at the Undertaker. Bleeping out the words is not suitable for kids like me. I looked up at the clock on the wall which was an old timey coo coo clock that a little bird would pop out every time it struck 12. It was currently 8:15. My bedtime was usually around nine but since it was the summer and Grandpa didn't have a bedtime set for me I could fall asleep whenever I pleased. But my mom had a strict bedtime for me during the school year so by the time 8:45 rolled around I started to get drowsy.

The wrestling program ended after I had dozed off on the couch. The rain had sounded peaceful and the thunder was beginning to become a soft crackle as the storm was beginning to pass over us. I was rudely awakened by the front door being slammed right open and Grandpa coming in huffing and puffing very hard. I sat up on the couch and could hear the bird of the coo-coo clock going off. It was precisely midnight. Grandpa hobbled inside the house removed his raincoat and placed it on the hook close to the door. His boots were covered in mud and his long white beard was drenched from the water. On top of his head, I could see a small amount of blood starting to slide down his face.

My heart raced as I ran over quickly to him. "Grandpa," I said in a squeaky voice, "are you okay?"

"I'm fine my boy," he told me, patting me firmly on the shoulder. "Just a little winded is all."

"But you're bleeding." I pointed up towards his bald head.

He gave me a startled look as he raised his shaky hands to his head. He touched where the blood was coming out from and winced. He looked at it for quite some time before whipping it on the side of his pants. He looked at me and smiled, "Oh it's nothing. Just bumped my dang head on one of the beacons inside the barn. Had to take a few things up to the upper level. Couldn't let them get wet. I'm fine."

"What things?" I asked. I had a strange feeling that he was keeping something from me and that was unlike Grandpa. He always told me that honesty would keep me out of trouble. And something was troubling in his eyes and his voice.

"Just somethings my boy, nothing for you to be concerned about. Now then tell me who won the last fight." Grandpa started making his way towards the bathroom.

"Oh, I fell asleep before it was over, I'm sorry."

Grandpa gave a little chuckle and said, "That's alright, your mama has kept you on that strict schedule for bed and that's because she got it from your grandpa. Like father like daughter."

Grandpa started shuffling some items around in the drawers and took out some peroxide. He splashed a little in his hand then proceeded to pat it on his head as if it was aftershave. He sharply sucked air through his teeth as he placed two bandaids on his cut. He walked out of the bathroom and patted me on the shoulder again with another chuckle.

"Now how's about we both get some rest tonight? It's been a very long day for this old fool."

I pushed a small smile at him and nodded my head. He hugged me, softly pushing me towards my bedroom. As I got undressed I listened to the rain that was still softly coming down. Trying to hear that odd mechanical noise I heard earlier, but the sound was gone. Just the soft pitter-patter of the rain that hit the roof of the house. I got in bed and lay there for quite some time. Thinking about those weird red and white flashings coming from the barn. There were no lights in the barn that I know of. I started to wonder if that mechanical noise was coming from the barn. That sound of a train screeching down its tracks. I knew Grandpa would be going into town the next day. Thursday was always his time to head into town for groceries and other supplies he needed around the house and his field. Tomorrow I would tell him that I wanted to stay at home while he went to run his errands and while he would be gone I would check out the barn for myself.

They always say curiosity killed the cat, sometimes I wonder how close I could have been to being that cat. Sometimes I wonder why I hadn't just left the stuff for the adults to handle. Sometimes I wonder if those things below my grandfather's field remember me after all these years.

I wonder.

***

I woke up to the smell of sausage and eggs being cooked. I got out of bed to get dressed. I made sure to put on some clothes and shoes that I wouldn't mind getting dirty while I did my exploration. After I was dressed I went into the kitchen where Grandpa had been humming a soft tune. My stomach made a loud rumble, making my grandfather stop humming.

"Good morning my boy," Grandpa said, still looking down at the sausage that had been sizzling madly on the pan.

"Morning," I said cheerfully.

"Sleep okay last night?"

"Slept like a log."

My grandfather chuckled, "Good, good," he started to place two sausage links onto my plate which already had scrambled eggs on it with a touch of my favorite, pancake syrup drizzled on top of it. Two pieces of toast popped out of the toaster. He picked one up and placed it on the plate. "Here you go, hope you're hungry."

"Starving," I told him. Which was the truth. I took the plate from the counter and over to the table where he would join me.

We scarfed down our breakfast as if it was the last meal on Earth. After we finished he collected our plates and took them to the sink. As he rinsed and cleaned our plates he asked me if I wanted to join him going into town. I opened my mouth to say sure until I remembered what I had already planned. When I told him that I just wanted to stay here Grandpa turned off the sink and then looked over to me while he dried his hands off with a rag.

"You sure," he asked me. "It might take me a while to come back home. Might have to run to College Station for a few extra things."

"I'm sure grandpa. I kind of just wanted to play by the pond for a little bit. Maybe chop up a few snakes and whatnot."

Whatnot? I thought to myself. I've never used that word before and I hoped he didn't find any suspicion in my voice. Luckily he didn't and gave me a big ol smile.

"You just be careful that there ain't any copperheads out there. Make sure to keep your cell phone with you just in case something should happen. You call 911 first then call my cell number. You got my number, don't you?"

I nodded my head. He walked over to me and patted my shoulder.

"Then I'll be back in a few hours. You have fun and… whatnot." Grandpa laughed to himself as he grabbed his key from the bowl on the table next to the door and walked out.

I went up to the window and watched as he got into his pickup truck. He started backing up the driveway and drove away into town. I looked over to the barn and started to feel butterflies in my stomach. I was beginning to feel overwhelmed with the feeling of anxious excitement. I went into my room to grab my backpack. I dumped everything that was in it onto my bed and then walked over to my desk. On it was a pocket knife that Grandpa gave me as an early birthday present. The handle was shaped like a miniature elephant's tusk that was gold. I pressed the small button in the center and out popped the sharp knife. I closed it before placing it in my pack along with a flashlight. I went out of my room and over to the front door of the house. I took a deep breath in, opened the door, and walked out.

The ground was still pretty muddy from last night's rain. With a clear sky, the sun beaming down made everything feel wet and sticky. Small beads of sweat already started to sprout from my forehead. I walked across the gravel driveway and just a little further down from the house, I was standing right in front of the barn doors. I raised the latch and opened the right side of the door just a bit for me to squeeze through. The smell of hay wafted heavily into my nose. There was a bit of sunlight that came through a small square of a hole on the upper level of the barn. I swung my pack around to reach in and take out the flashlight.

I didn't quite know what I was looking for but I figured I would know what it would be. Something probably big with big lights, possibly LED. I checked the first stable only to find a small bucket sitting on top of a pile of hay. Nothing. I went across to the next stable which was empty. Nothing. I tried remembering those lights that seemed to consume Grandpa before he went in. I went to the far end of the barn. Still nothing. I surveyed every square inch of the barn with my flashlight and was about to call it quits, head back into the house to hop on my Game Boy when something caught my eye. It glimmered on the ground near the far corner of the barn. As I walked up to it I saw it was a small pull handle that was poorly covered up with hay.

Just a few inches away from the pull handle I started to hear the ground beneath shift and change in sound, as if whatever was beneath my feet was something hollow. I got down on my hands and knees to brush the hay away from the handle to see it was some sort of door that you find in the sides of houses that lead down into a cellar. I went to the side of the handle and began to raise it. It was heavy enough that I had to jump back to my feet just to lift it. Just about when it was nearly open the handle swung out my hands with a brute force and I could feel a cool gush of air wash on out from below me. I shined my flashlight into what was now a hole in the ground to see stone stairs that led into blackness down below.

I swallowed, feeling my hands grow clammy. My eyes were wide from the sheer fact that it looked as if the stairs continued down forever. I was beginning to take a step forward into my newfound discovery then paused right where I was at. What exactly was I doing? As a kid, you would think I would find something like this to be terrifying. Like something out of a horror movie that you watch as the character does something stupid and you say,

No don't go down there. You'll be sorry. But my curiosity was much stronger than my fear. Yet I still dropped my bag on the ground and fished out my pocket knife. I placed it into my back pocket, zipped up my bag then threw it over my shoulders once more. Again I took a deep breath. Trying to be as brave as my grandpa, took one step down those stone stairs and continued forward. I had to know what was down there. Why? Because I was very curious.

I walked down the stone stairs and could start to feel a cool breeze coming from down below. I glanced back up towards the entrance and could only see a small faint light coming from above. I had a horrible thought. What if the door latch closed? I shook the thought away, thinking that if there was a tornado that just came through that's when I should worry. But it was a bright sunny day so the possibilities of that were non-existent. I needed to be brave so I journeyed on.

It felt as if the stairs just kept going and going. Leading to God knows what. The air was suddenly becoming richer. The cool breeze had begun to slow and as I was drawing closer to the bottom I started to hear a faint noise. It sounded to me like soft jazz music or the kind of music you would hear in an elevator. And there was something else I could hear but it was much too faint. Then I could finally see the bottom coming up.

As I reached the bottom, the ground was made of tiles that seemed busted, cracked, and ancient. I stood at the bottom of the stairs, mouth ajar, eyes wide as I could not believe what I was seeing. I had somehow ended up in some kind of abandoned shopping center. It was like a giant mall of some sort. It sort of reminded me of the Galleria Mall in Houston where my mom would always take me to do some school shopping. Pillars were made out of small white tiles that stretched up to a ceiling with single hanging lights. Although some of the lights were missing, the rest that were still intact were on. An escalator that went to a second level had been broken in half. Some stores had security gates closed for anyone entering. The smell was that of a used bookstore. Soft jazz music echoed throughout this odd mysterious place along with the sound of... People? A crowd of people who were conversing with one another had been coming from the other side of the shopping center.

I wanted to shout out a hello, yet something about that seemed like a very bad idea. I didn't know if it was my gut intuition that was saying that, but I listened nonetheless. I went towards the sound where I could hear people talking and laughing with each other. As I drew closer to the broken down escalator I started to hear footsteps coming from behind me drawing closer. I spun around quickly to see who was approaching, only to find nothing there. Even the footsteps had stopped dead. I rubbed my eyes with the back of my hand that was holding the flashlight. I switched the light to my other hand and could feel the dampness of it from my sweat. I turned back around towards the sound of people when I noticed something just a few meters away from me.

A small ball of light seemed to be floating in mid-air. Slowly, dreamily droning up and down. I continued towards it, not noticing that my hand was beginning to shake. Like how my grandpa's hand was shaking when I told him that his head was bleeding. I could feel some sort of heat radiating off this ball of light as I drew closer. I reached out with my hand which was not holding the flashlight to the ball of light. As I was about to touch it the weird cotton ball of light disappeared. Suddenly more balls of light started emerging out of thin air. It looked as if it was guiding me towards something. Perhaps the voices of the people I was starting to hear grew louder.

"Hey," a whisper of a boy came from the side of me that gave me a small startle.

I flashed the light towards the sound that was coming from inside one of the stores. There was a sign on top that read *Alex* above the entrance. I walked closer to the store. My mouth had become so dry that I wished I would have packed a bottle of water. I swallowed the bit of spit that I could and that helped some.

When I got to the security gates I noticed that it was some sort of clothing department. There were five mannequins towards the front of the store wearing faded shirts and jeans. Two adult sized mannequins to the right and three kid sized ones next to them. A certain eerie feeling washed over me thinking that the mannequins were alive, just standing there watching me as I looked in, shining my light everywhere trying to see what had called out to me.

"He-hello?" I said feebly.

I waited for anything to call out to me but I heard nothing at all. There came a soft breeze on the back of my neck that made me quickly turn around. Again I came to find nothing was behind me. When I turned back around to look back into the store I noticed that one of the kid sized mannequins at the far end was gone. My eyes widened and I slowly started to back away from the store. Thinking that I had enough of what was going on and feeling my bravery fall short, I turned to run back towards the stairs that led me down to this weird ghostly place. But when I got back to where the stairs were they were gone too. As if the stairs were never there to begin with. I know for a fact that where I had been standing should have been the place I came in from, but... there was nothing. The sound of jazz music seemed to have increased and now I could hear a woman softly singing overhead.

I scratched my head furiously as I turned back to where I ran from. There was that single ball of light yet again just droning up and down. I started to suspect that maybe it would lead me to an exit. Praying that it would lead me to an exit. Praying that I didn't make some sort of horrible mistake of coming down here.

Promise me you'll stay right here, my grandpa's voice ringing in my head from last night. Some promise I had fucked up.

I walked back up to the ball of light and again it disappeared, causing the other ball of light to appear in a straight line that eventually curved to the left just a little down the way. As I walked past the Alex store I kept my eyes straight on the floating balls of light. Growing closer to the sounds of people and jazz music. The music seemed old, like something from the forties or fifties. The trumpets were low and a bass guitar strummed slowly and steadily. The singer sounded like a black lady as she sang:

> *Baby come on down,*
>
> *Take me down to that place,*
>
> *Ohh baby don't make me sad,*
>
> *Yeah baby we'll be alright,*
>
> *Just fine darling if you come on down*

I surprisingly found a certain comfort in her voice. It was like listening to my mom sing as she used to do whenever she would do some cleaning around the house. Humming some sort of sweet melody to herself.

When I reached the corner where the ball of lights started to turn I saw that this part of the shopping center was completely lit up. A huge crystal chandelier was suspended that was caked with dust. This entire section of the shopping mall didn't look like a shopping mall at all. Instead, it appeared to be some sort of huge party room. The floor had switched from worn down tiles to red and yellow carpet. There were patches on the ground, exposing the hard cement that lay underneath. Two rows of huge tiled pillars continued down to the very end. To my right, I noticed a directory board that seemed to have mapped out the entire place I was in.

I walked up to the directory hoping to find some sort of secret exit I could walk out of and back towards my grandpa's house. What was Grandpa even doing with this place underneath his land? Why was he trying to keep it a secret? Both questions felt uneasy to me and I was not sure if I wanted them to be answered anymore. Standing in front of the directory I could see the plastic covering had been ripped out. The map of this place had been scribbled over with black marker with words that might have seemed to be warnings. I traced to where I had come in, I saw the word Alex was written over one of the stores near the broken down escalator. Next to it was the name Diane, followed by Terry. When I reached the corner that I was at the word Dance Hall was written in red instead of the black that was used for those mysterious names. Just past the Dance Hall read: The Sleeping Lair. I didn't like the sound of that one at all. I started to wonder if these balls of light were steering me clear of that part of the shopping center. Maybe these cotton balls of light were put here by Grandpa. But why?

I came back to where I was and traced with my eyes down the Dance Hall. At the end, I could see a huge X in black markings on the right side and left side. In the very center in red, it said: *Push the second tile from the bottom, DO NOT MAKE A SOUND!* The center had been circled madly and beyond that was nothing more. I checked down the party hall to see the ball of lights had gone down in a straight line leading to a gigantic wall that looked to be covered by a huge velvet drape.

Seeing that I would not be going anywhere towards what was known as the sleeping lair, I swung my backpack off my shoulders, turned off my flashlight to conserve my battery life, and placed it back into my bag. As I put my bag over my shoulders I heard something bouncing its way towards me. As I looked towards the shopping center part where I previously came down a small blue rubber ball was bouncing its way towards me. It rolled until it hit my feet and stopped right where it was at. I studied the ball, reminding me of the one I used to play with back when I was younger at my old elementary school. The ball had a name written on it with a black marker, Diane. When I looked up to see who or what had tossed this ball my way I saw nothing but the few dust from the ground that the ball had kicked up. Then, very faintly I started to hear a shushing noise.

"Shh, shh, shh," as if whatever was causing this noise didn't want to be seen, or as I would later find out, didn't want to be caught.

Without thinking I started walking down the dance hall in a panicky hurry. Passing the giant balls of light that's leading me towards the wall covered by the velvet drapes. Drawing closer to the sound of the smooth jazz music along with what I can hear from the group of people. Their conversations were coming in more fluently now that I could pick up a few words that were being spoken. Now as I approached the drapes I could without a doubt know that these people along with the jazz music were behind the curtain.

When I reached the end of the Dance Hall I could see the huge drape that had been covered by a thick coat of dust and dirt. Before I reached out to see what lay behind it, I looked to my sides and was dumbstruck. On both my sides were two push doors with a sign above them that read: EXIT. I placed my hands to my sides looking to my left then to my right and back to my left. I suddenly remembered the directory that had two huge X's that crossed out. Another one of those gut intuitions started to tell me that something about those doors seemed to be some sort of trick, or perhaps even a trap.

The light from the chandelier started to flicker before they slowly started to dim. The balls of light that led me down the party hall started to fade away one by one. Anxiety started rising as I put my attention back to the drape ahead of me. I looked for a parting that separated the drape but it had just been one huge drape that covered this humongous wall. The dance hall was now starting to get darker and I could hear once more the sound of that rubber ball bouncing its way towards me. I didn't want to turn around to see if something was after me. I could feel a presence starting to grow closer and closer. I dropped to my knees to start raising the drape from its bottom. A wave of terror rose over me, thinking that a cold hand would brush the back of my neck, pulling me away by whatever was approaching from behind me, taking me away and doing something to me that I just couldn't imagine or even dragging me to that Sleeping Lair.

Finally, I could start to see the stone wall that lay behind the velvet drape. It was completely smooth except for five tiles in different colors. From the bottom to the top, it went yellow, black, green, white, and red. Trying to remember which tile I needed to push the light behind me was almost diminished. The rubber ball was just a few feet away, growing louder as it kept bouncing and almost started to sound like heavy footsteps. I heard, "*Shh shh,*" behind me, as if it was coming from above my head. Then that shushing sound reminded me that I needed to push the second tile from the bottom. I pushed the black tile. There came a sound of a door being unlocked to my right but the light had almost darkened the entire room. I got back to my feet, running my hands across the smooth stone wall for some sort of door.

It was now completely dark and the bouncing of the ball had switched. What I could hear now was the sound of someone heavily breathing. I finally found the indentation in the wall and pushed it forward. The wall opened just enough for me to slip through. Once I was through I closed the door behind me, pressing my back against it with all the force I had.

I stood there panting like I had just finished running a marathon. When I believed that the coast was clear, I bent over with my hands on my knees. I looked up to find myself now in some sort of long corridor. At the end was another door that was slightly ajar with the sound of people conversing, laughing, and shouting along with the jazz music that was now just ahead of me. Coming right behind that door. A bright green neon sign, which was the only light in this oblong hallway, came on right above the door with a name on it that made me feel very cold and uncomfortable. The sign said: *Desmond.* It was my name. There came a low hum from the sign that echoed down the corridor.

I stood straight up to continue forward into this mess I got myself into. Desperately hope that I can get myself out of it. The walls were made out of huge white bricks and the floor was made out of hardwood. The odd thing was my footsteps didn't seem to match with what was below me. It was as if I was wearing boots as my feet made a hard clicking noise. The noise of the jazz music grew louder as it was coming to an end. Right before I stood in front of the door I looked up at my name on the sign. The hum of it was dimming, making a sound like it was running low on power. I began to hear hoots and hollers, whistles and applause as the jazz music had finally concluded. The lady that had been singing was thanking the audience and telling them how wonderful they'd been tonight.

Tonight? I thought to myself. When I left my grandpa's house it was only ten forty-five in the morning. I licked my lips as I began to reach for the door. My hand had started to tremble yet again as I placed it on the door.

When I opened it with a quick force, I could feel my heart sink. My eyes grew wide, and every inch of my body burst out into goosebumps. The room, which I heard without a doubt playing music and hearing people talking at a huge party, was empty. Two light bulbs that hung in the center of the room reflected how ancient it was here. The neon sign had shut off as if someone or something had flipped the switch. I took a few steps into the room, flabbergasted by this whole bizarre situation. The door behind me crept and creaked its way shut. I jumped when I heard the click of the latch securing the door shut. The air in the room seemed thin, not because of how scared I was now, but the aura of this place seemed to be... off. There is no explanation for why this was but I could feel it. That is until I noticed a single picture frame at the end of the room.

I swung my backpack around yet again to take out my flashlight. I turned it on to study the room. It reminded me of an old club VIP room. The floor was made of yellow carpet covered in dirt. It seemed there used to be wallpaper but had now started to peel away. Tables on each side of the room with chairs that were either pushed into the tables or had been flipped over. Below the picture frame was a stage with two guitar stands, a drum set, and a microphone stand in the center. I continued down the room to where the picture frame was. A golden plaque was pinned just below the picture frame. I stepped onto the stage and it gave a loud groan as if it was going to collapse beneath me.

The golden plaque read: *The Grand Opening Ceremony of the Marquee's Galleria, Owner Lewis Banks. June 20th, 1980.*

My jaw was about ready to hit the floor after reading that as I took a long look at the picture frame. Lewis Banks, my grandfather, the father of my mother, owned this phantasmagoric place. In the picture was my grandfather in the middle surrounded by a huge group of people while holding a small baby. Next to him was a young black woman who reminded me of how flappers used to dress back in the twenties. Her hair was short and she had her arms wrapped around my grandfather's neck. She had a gorgeous smile as her teeth seemed to glow from the snap of the picture. Next to her was a white man with an electric bass guitar raised high into the air. Those two must have been the jazz players I previously heard. And the group of people must have been also what I had been hearing as well.

But something else caught my eye in this picture. On the opposite side of my grandfather were three children, one girl and two boys, who looked almost out of place with the whole picture. The girl who looked no older than six or seven was Asian, one of the boys who had to be my age was tall and had blonde hair and had his arms crossed around his chest, and the other boy who could have been the same age as the Asian girl was also white but was completely bald. All three children had a poker face, not smiling one bit. They looked like they didn't want to take a picture at all. For some reason, I pointed at the girl in the picture and then to the two other boys and thought, *Diane, Alex, Terry?* I wasn't completely sold that those were their names, but something told me that it was. Then I got closer to the picture and studied the baby my grandfather was holding. *Mom?*

I grabbed the picture with my free hand and started to pull it off the wall. Not knowing that there had been a string right behind it, a door to my right had sprung open and gave me a good startle that made me rip the picture off the string. I cocked my head a little as I shined my flashlight towards the door. A light started coming from whatever was behind that door and it began to grow brighter. Like a secret sun was beginning to rise. I began to look at the picture once more before I stowed it away into my bag to take back to Grandpa as I had a few questions for him until I noticed that something was written on the back of the frame.

Left, right, three doors down, quietly pass the green door, left, right, up the stairs, close the door behind you! Do not wake them up!

My eyes lit up. What I held in my hands looked to be some sort of directions to get out of here. I swallowed hard as I studied the directions once more. I placed the picture frame into my backpack before stepping off the stage to head out the door that had opened up for me. As I approached the door I heard one of the chairs begin to move as it made a soft click touching the table at the far end of the room. I quickly flashed my light towards that sound and saw something quickly go underneath the table.

"Who's there?" I asked softly.

I started to hear the voice of a young boy breathing heavily and saying, "*You shouldn't be here. Don't run, or you'll wake them.*"

My heart was rapping against my chest. I licked my lips and said, "Who is them? Who are you?"

Silence. Even the heavy breathing had stopped. Until another chair started to move towards the wall and another chair next to it flipped over. Whatever was underneath the table was getting closer to me. There came another voice of a boy, one much older than the first voice I heard saying, "*They are the ones who didn't make it out. The ones that slumber because their souls have left them. The lights that lead you here… are their souls. The ones that slumber want to keep you here,*

Desmond. Your grandfather left us here to rot. Left us here because he failed. Left us. Left us. Left us. LEFT US!"

Those voices… could they possibly be the two boys from the picture? Alex and Terry? The table closest to me had been hoisted into the air and flew across the room like a man in rage flipping it over. I turned quickly and ran out of the room. The door behind me slammed shut and I could see the balls of light that guided me here were once again right in front of me, only this time they were floating up and down much faster this time. Slowly glowing from white to red, then to green. Like the lights I had witnessed from inside Grandpa's house when Grandpa went out into the barn last night during the storm.

"Hurry Desmond," a cry of a young girl that echoed all around me.

I looked all around me to find this voice. A sudden image came to my head. The picture on the wall with the kids standing right next to Grandpa at the grand opening of his mall. "Diane," I called out, "Diane is that you?"

"Yes. Alex and Terry want them to wake up to keep you here! Don't run! They like it when you run."

My eyes looked down the hall I was in and proceeded forward in quick steps. Trying my best to remember the directions from the picture frame as I was too afraid to pull it out of my backpack. I came to the first intersection and looked both ways as the balls of lights went in both directions. I suddenly remembered, Left! I turned and as I came up to one of the balls of lights my arm made contact with it as it gave me a sharp sensation of being shocked. A big mistake I had just made. The balls of lights went from Red, Green, and White, to completely black. They stopped floating up and down as they were now motionless.

I continued forward and came to yet again another intersection. Right! I turned down the next hall and saw four doors on my right with the last door that looked different from the others. It was much bigger and was painted green instead of the brown the other doors had. I quickly walked down the hall trying not to touch the black balls of light, until I reached the last brown door when one of the black balls floated towards me. I tried to maneuver around it but had no luck. It brushed my shoulder, giving me another sharp shocking pain that coursed down my body. Then the balls of light hovered in the air.

An excruciating loud alarm started to blare over me that made me cup my hands to my ears. The giant green door started to slowly creep open. I tried walking forward and suddenly felt my body grow cold as I stood right in front of the once-closed green door. Inside the room I could see hundreds of people standing shoulder to shoulder with their eyes shut, hibernating and not moving a single muscle. Their bodies were gray and there were dust and cobwebs over their heads down to their feet. I was ready to scream before the alarm started to shout slowly, "IN...TRU...DER! IN... TRU... DER! IN... TRU... DER!

That's when my brain finally screamed to my feet to move! I walked past the door and wanted to run, until the voice of the little girl shouted into my head, *don't run! They like it when you run.*

Finally, I came to another section and was too scared to remember which way to go. I threw my backpack over my shoulders, opened it, and took out the picture frame. I checked the back and went over the directions again. And that's when I heard a huge crowd screaming my name. Beckoning out to me in unison. I returned my attention to the directions on the back of the frame yet again and finally saw which way I needed to go, I was close.

As I began to turn down the left hallway the black balls of light started to form a wall in front of me. Blocking me in so I couldn't continue forward. Then the balls of light started to push their way towards me. I backed away from them, the spirits that were left here by my grandpa. The crowd of people shouted my name once more and I could see the once sleeping people standing at the far end of the hall, with their eyes still shut. I was trapped. I was going to die here. I was going to become a rotting spirit because I was too curious to know what was down here.

"Desmond!!" A new voice cried out to me. A familiar voice. I quickly turned and saw it was my grandpa, he had been sweating hard and his face was completely drenched. "Desmond, quickly come this way! We gotta get out of here!"

I ran to him and he gave me a gripping hug and checked to see if I was alright. After two seconds he took me by the arm and started guiding me down the clear hallway. We ran until we came to a dead end. He fell on the wall looking for something that I couldn't see for myself. I checked behind us and saw the black balls of light floating right behind the crowd of sleeping people. Then, one by one, the crowd started to open their eyes. Their eyes shined a bright green and they all started to open their mouths as they made a piercing scream. Their screams started to become a grueling chant.

"Left us! Left us! Left us! Left us!"

The black balls of light started coming towards Grandpa and me when I felt Grandpa place his hand on my shoulder.

"Come on!" He shouted.

There was now an open spot where the wall used to be and I could see there were stone stairs that were leading up. We went through and Grandpa was struggling to shut the wall behind us.

"Help me, Desmond! We can't let them get out! Alex and Terry have put a curse in this place and if any of them or the ones chasing us should get out then it could be very cataclysmic."

I got to the side of my grandpa and started to push the wall. It felt as if it was trying to move a stone elephant. The chants of the crowd were now closer than ever as the wall was slowly beginning to close. A gray arm reached out from the other side and began to claw at my grandpa's arm. Grandpa screamed and cursed until the wall finally was closed. He pushed me up the stairs as we made our way up. We ran until my legs started to feel like wet noodles. A small light started to appear in front of me, making me run much faster.

We reached the top and I tripped on the last step and fell into a pile of hay. My chest heaved in and out as I tried to catch my breath. I turned to my back and pushed myself far from the hole I just come out of as Grandpa came out wheezing. He went over to the side of the hole once he was out and slammed the cellar-like door closed. He collapsed to his knees and breathed just as heavily as I was. He looked over at me. My face was full of sweat and my eyes had tears coming down them. Grandpa crawled his way toward me, pulled me by my shoulder, and hugged me as tightly as he ever had.

"What was that?!" I cried.

Without releasing me he said, "Something that I wish I could get rid of. The mistake from my past. I'm just so happy you're alright."

"Diane, she's the one that helped me escape." Just thinking of her voice sent a small shiver down my spine.

I finally hugged my grandfather back and wept heavily into his shoulders. "Promise me you'll keep this a secret. No one can know about my past mistakes. Not even your mother. She can't know about the three kids that were her adopted siblings." Grandpa had let me go and we looked deeply into each other's eyes. His eyes seemed worn down, showing more of his old age than I have ever seen, "Alex and Terry grew jealous of your mother and I didn't know that they came from a lineage that practiced with dark magic. The devil's works. They killed Diane inside my mall and later killed themselves after opening up the mall. Placing a curse on them and everyone that was in it. By the time I got there, it was too late. The mall started to sink into the ground like quicksand, only leaving behind the stairway to enter and exit that hallway. It's my responsibility to keep everything in there locked up. It's my responsibility to keep it a secret. That's why I had my land, my barn, and my house to cover it up. Can I trust you to keep it a secret? That way no one will unleash the horrors that lay down below?"

I looked at him, completely dumbfounded by everything he told me. My mouth was dry as it hung open. I pressed my lips together and gave him a slight nod.

He hugged me again as I looked over his shoulder. Looking at the cellar-like door and at that time I could have sworn I still saw the flashing lights from the night before. But when he let me go no lights were flashing at all. I still wonder if Alex, Terry, and Diane think about me as they lay underneath Grandpa's field to this day. But from my past experiences, I know better than to not let my curiosity get the best of me. Not anymore.

MR. STRANGER

ON A COOL LATE EVENING, the sun sank into the Earth giving the last bit of light, turning the sky from a bright fiery orange to a soft purple, then finally to black. The moon replaced the sun for what little light it had to offer as a couple named Othello and Patricia were leaving work together, and heading home after a long and stressful day.

The couple both worked for a motel and cafe called The Sun Rise. Othello was the head chef and for Patricia, she was a server. On nights such as this one where the college football rage between Alabama and Texas A&M went on, the people of Franklin, Texas often chose The Sun Rise as their go-to spot to catch the game, have a few drinks, and have something tasty to eat. Once it was time to close, the couple were the first ones out into the parking lot, getting into their car, and sitting there for a brief moment in complete silence, making a mental note that the day was now over after a ten-long hour shift. Finally Othello in the driver seat starts the car and drives it out of the parking lot to head home.

The radio which had been playing The Passenger by the Deftones was coming to an end and a radio broadcaster came on.

"That was the Deftones, on WKTT Franklin's Hard Rock Station," the broadcaster said, "In local news, 27-year-old Marcee Tank is still missing and the person in charge of Nigel Tank's murder has still yet to be caught. Authorities are saying this could be the works of The Alphabet stalker who has been killing and kidnapping a wide variety of victims. Police say if you have any information on the couple contact your local sheriff's department. In weather-" Othello turned off the radio giving it a quiet, *Click*.

"Just play the damn songs why don't ya," he said, rolling down his window and spitting out some phlegm, exposing the cool night air into their vehicle.

"I was listening to that," Patricia said.

"Well now you ain't," Othello said smirking.

The car then began to sputter and slowly decreased in speed. A light from the instrument panel began to flash telling the couple they were out of gas.

"God dammit Patricia," Othello said smacking the steering wheel, "I thought you put gas in here this morning."

"I did!" Patricia said blatantly.

"You fucking liar! If you did then why are we stopped-"

Patricia raised her hands to her boyfriend. "Othello please calm down, remember what the doctor said about your blood pressure."

Patricia could see the vein on the side of her boyfriend's head begin to rapidly pulse and he could start to feel it. He took a deep breath in and exhaled it slowly.

"Alright, alright," Othello said, with a nonchalant tone. "Well, we should try calling for Triple-A. Is your phone still on because mine is dead?"

Patricia reached into her purse and pulled out her cell phone. It too was also dead.

"Well, fuck me." Othello said, "There's a gas tank in the trunk. We can walk to the nearest store. I think it's a Texaco which is about 5 miles that way." He pointed forward down the road which seemed to have no end and stretched on forever into a dark abyss.

"Maybe I should stay here with the car," Patricia suggested.

"Like hell you will. I ain't walking there and back by myself."

"Is someone scared?" Patricia taunted.

"Bitch, just get out and get the gas tank and let's go. I'm done arguing."

He got out of the car and popped open the trunk. Patricia got out and went around the back grabbed a five-gallon gas tank and closed the trunk. She walked up to the side of Othello as he locked the car and they began their walk.

About 2 miles down their pace slowed down as hunger began to be mixed with how exhausted they already were. That's when Patricia noticed a car with its hazards blinking on the side of the road.

"You think that person would be willing to give us a ride?" Patricia asked groggily.

"I was just thinking the same thing," Othello said.

They sluggishly approached a car that was blasting Queen's Bohemian Rhapsody. Othello looked back at Patricia as she waved her hands towards the car, mouthing the words, *Go, GO!* He turned back and started towards the driver's side door.

Othello could see a man wearing a white button-down shirt with a red vest over it. The man was also wearing a scally cap and was softly beating his hands on the steering wheel to the rhythm of the song.

"Excuse me, sir?" Othello said, but not loud enough for the man to hear him. The music was just too loud. Othello looked back at Patricia. This time she made a fist and began knocking at an imaginary window as she was trying to signal that to Othello.

He turned back around to the car window and gave it a slight, *tap tap*. The man in the car turned his head almost giving him whiplash and stared at the man at his car door. Othello pointed a finger downwards trying to have the man roll down the window to which the man did along with turning off his radio.

"Excuse me, sir, I'm sorry to bother you." Othello began to say. He looked at the man's face trying to see his features and whether or not he was friendly or some whacked-out druggie. They had many of those in the small town of Franklin where you could always tell what kind of drug was their poison. But the man had a friendly face and almost one that could be punchable. He calmly smiled softly, exposing the whitest of teeth Othello had ever seen. They were bright enough to be the stars on the blackest of nights. It also seemed a bit creepy to Othello only seeing the man's teeth in the dark vehicle.

"How can I help you, sir?" The man said in a soothing and collective voice.

"I hate to ask you this but me and my girl just got off of work and our car ran out of gas." Othello pointed at Patricia and he continued. "We were hoping to get a ride to the Texaco just down the road and back to our car which is, like, 2 miles that way." He tossed his hand behind him and the man's bright green eyes followed Othello's hand and then back to Othello.

"I have ten dollars I could give you, bro. We're both just really tired and want to get home."

The man in the car who never once lost that big luminous smile studied Othello then shifted his eyes at Patricia briefly then back to Othello. The wind whistled throughout the night as a small pause between the two men caught them at a standstill. The man unlocked his car and pointed his head letting them know that he agreed to do this for them.

"Good man," Othello said, tapping the roof of the man's car two times. "You're a damn good man. Come on, baby."

He opened the door behind the driver's side to let Patricia in and closed it for her. He ran to the other side and got in the backseat with her.

"Bless you, sir," Patricia said. She examined the car and how clean it was and even smelled fresh. Almost like it was a brand-new car.

Othello reached into his back pocket to take out the ten-dollar bill and handed it to the man. The man waved his hand at it.

"No need for that sir," The man said. "Just doing what's right."

Othello is dumbstruck by how gracious this man is. He thought, *If we were some other folks, this car would be robbed and he would be dead.*

"You said the Texaco gas station, Correct?" The man said robotically.

"Yep, that's the one," Othello said.

The man nodded his head, turned his hazard signals off, and began to drive forward.

They drove for a good three minutes until all three could see the bright red and black sign which read TEXACO. Patricia noticed that the man did not show any effort to slow down to turn into the gas station.

"Yeah, it's uh." Patricia started to say, "It's this one coming up to your left."

The man's eyes were still forward and maintaining his speed. Patricia looked at Othello with eyes that said *Say something to him*.

"Hey buddy, you're fixing to pass it," Othello said.

"Hm?" The man said looking at the couple through his rearview mirror. "Oh, you don't want to go there. I know a better gas station with cheaper gas."

"But we just need to get a little bit of gas, and we didn't want to be gone from our car that long," Patricia said.

"Well," the man said, looking at the road again. "I really want a slushy from this gas station that we're going to, so two birds with one stone, am I right?" And let out a small laugh

The couple in the back did not say anything and watched as they passed the Texaco. They stared at each other knowing that the next gas station was a lot further away. Suspicion grew between the two and became even worse as the man slowed down on pitch black road flipped his blinker on and turned right.

"Hey man where are you going?" Othello asked, nearly shouting. The man paid no attention to him and continued straight. Patricia grasped the side of Othello's arm in fear now.

"HELLO! Earth to dipshit." Othello ranted. Patricia shakes his arm now beginning to breathe rapidly.

"HEY ASSHOLE!"

"Please don't yell in my car." The man finally said, with a firm tone. It was much heavier than how he was originally speaking.

"Well, where the fuck are you going?" Othello shouted. "There ain't nothing this way and we just told you we didn't want to be gone from our car for that long!"

"I said," The man accelerating his car, "Don't. Yell. In. My. Car."

"Then where the fuck are you taking us. Just turn back around and we'll walk back from Texaco you fucking psycho!" Othello screamed.

"Othello please," Patricia said, shaking his arm.

He took away his arm from her grasp. "Shut up, Patricia!"

The man smiled as he slammed his foot on the brakes as the couple in the back went face-first into the driver and passenger seat's headrests. In a dazed confusion, Patricia could hear her boyfriend shouting and swearing.

"YOU MOTHERFUCKER! YOU BROKE MY GODDAMN NOES!" Othello proclaims while holding his nose as his hand becomes consumed in his blood.

"I said," The man said; locking his doors, opening up his center console, taking out a 9mm revolver, turning and facing Othello, and shooting him in the head spraying brain matter on the back windshield. "Don't yell in my car."

Patricia screams and tries to open her door to escape the man's car but does not have any luck. She pounds her bare hand on the window leaving a bloody smear.

"Shut up or you'll be next!" The man said, pointing the gun at Patricia.

"Please sir," Patricia cried as mucus from her nose waterfalled along with her tears and sniffles, "Please don... Don't hur... Hurt muh-me." She puts her hands up shielding her face from the gun as the man removes his scally cap to reveal a large gash on the man's forehead as a strand of hair falls over it he brushes the strand out of his face and puts the gun in his side door.

"Get up here in the front with me and let's just cruise for a bit, okay?" The man said in his calm manner, like the first time the couple met him, putting his cap back on.

Patricia was confused about what to do but she did as the man instructed. While transitioning from the back seat to the front passenger side she glanced over at her dead boyfriend's body. Blood was oozing from the front and back of Othello's temple. His eyes were in the back of his head and mouth wide open in a stupified expression. She vomits near Othello's feet due to her nerves being shocked and this is the first time she's seen someone that was shot to death in person. She thought to herself that this was way worse than what they show in the movies or TV.

Much worse.

She climbs over the center console and sits in the passenger seat. The man had both hands on the steering wheel at ten and two with a great big luminous smile on his face that seemed to be competing for a brighter natural light with the waxing crescent moon that lingered in the sky. They sat in the car in silence with only the sound of the car's engine running. The man takes a deep breath as something crosses his mind, and looks at Patricia with the face of a man that just had a brilliant idea. Patricia wipes away the boogers that sat on the top of her lips and takes two quick breaths in.

"Are you going to kill me?" Patricia sniffled.

The man opens his center console again and grabs a small notebook along with an even smaller pencil. He began to scratch something off with the pencil. Patricia tried to see what it was but it was too dark for her to even get a glimpse at it.

"I don't know yet," the man said as he returned the notebook from where he took it out from. "We'll just have to see after our ride."

He puts the car in drive and continues forward. They sat in uncomfortable silence for ten minutes as the man kept driving and turned onto a dirt road. He finally broke the silence to ask her a question.

"That man in the back seat," The man started to say.

"His name was Othello." Patricia almost shouted but remembered what happened if she had raised her voice in this strange man's car and wiped her nose.

"Right, Othello. And he said your name was Patricia right."

This time she didn't say anything. The road that they were on began to turn into an open land with nothing on it from what Patricia could see. The land was flat with dirt rocks and loose gravel. The man drives up the land and turns around making a complete three hundred and sixty degrees. He cuts off his lights and exhales long and softly.

"Tonight is my lucky night I guess." The man says to himself, "Two couples in just three days, how wonderful." He begins to laugh maniacally.

Patricia begins to cry and sniffle profusely. The man turns to Patricia with his great big smile.

"I'm almost done with my list, you want to see it?" The man asked with a ghastly tone. Patricia didn't say anything but the man brought out the small notebook again. It was a list of the alphabet with all of the letters crossed out between A and O. Patricia, now realizing what this man had planned and began pleading for her life.

"Now now dear. I'm not going to shoot you." The man said, taking his hands off the wheels and stroking Patricia's head. "But I will say this. I'm going to unlock my car and you're going to get out and run whichever direction you want. Now then," He takes his hands off her head and sets them back on the steering wheel. "Once I turn the headlights back on, that means you better run faster."

The man throws his head back and laughs heartily while he bangs his hands on his steering wheel to get him aroused and ready.

"And… GO!"

The car doors unlocked and Patricia without hesitation got out and ran to the east of the car. The darkness made everything harder to see and added with her crocodile tears it became even more of a struggle.

"Everyone thinks it's smarter to run in the direction my car isn't facing." The man says to himself as he cackles, turning his car to face the fleeing woman.

Patricia, not noticing a large tree branch where the man had planted there earlier that day trips over it and falls to the ground scraping skin off her knees and breaking her wrist. The man turned the headlights on Patricia as she lay there in agony holding on to her now numb wrist. She scurries to her feet and begins running again.

Thanks to the lights of the car she could see she had a good fifty yards before she could reach a wooden gate. The man began to accelerate his car catching up to her. Patricia then trips on her own feet and again falls to the ground. She turned around and saw the vehicle coming closer and closer. She turns back around as she drags herself onto the ground and then begins to feel the pressure of a tire crushing her foot and rolling up to her leg breaking every bone. She cries for someone to help her but the nearest house is a good nine miles away. Making this a perfect spot to hide the bodies as well.

The man began to reverse his car, centered his tire on Patricia's body, and drove forward snapping her waist bone and crushing her organs to finally flatten her head as her eyes popped out of her head.

The man clapped his hands and cheered as he placed his car in park. He took out the list again and gleefully scratched out the P on his list.

Two days later, the man went inside of a gas station and walked up to the slushy machine which had a sign on it saying out of order. He walked up to the front register and asked the cute cashier woman, who he had studied the name badge on her which read *Quinley* on it, about the slushy machine.

"Yeah sorry about that, sugar." The cute cashier said with a twang in her voice. "Machine has been busted for three days now. Should have someone coming to work on it soon."

"Aw shucks," the man said, snapping his fingers.

"There is a Texaco that's just down the road down yonder that has a machine still working, I believe." the cashier said, throwing her hand to her left.

The man smiled his luminous smile and he thanked her.

The cashier was watching the news as a report of a couple that had gone missing. The man shook his head at this news.

"What has the world come to these days?" The man asked.

"I know right?" The cashier sighed, "Damn shame about those people that have gone missing in the past few days. You make sure you stay careful out there Mister."

The man began walking out and stopped to turn around to the cashier with a dastardly grin to say.

"Just make sure you don't talk to any strangers and you should be fine." The strange man walks out of the gas station, laughing.

THE BREAKOUT

FROM ABOVE CAME A BLARE that sounded like a damn nuclear plant meltdown alarm. I sprung up quickly with anxiety and noticed I wasn't in my bed. I wasn't even home. I had been locked up in the Grimes County jail. And man being hungover was just the cherry on this shit ice cream. I *told* myself I shouldn't go out the previous night, yet I got trailer trash wasted and had another blackout. Guess this time I wasn't lucky enough to make it back home.

A tall black policeman standing at damn near six feet and four inches that was built like a brick house walked past me with his many rings jingling and jangling on the side of his hip. The officer, whose bright golden name badge read Lucas Bowers, was wearing a black cowboy hat that reminded me of someone who would wear that in the outlaw days. He stops right in front of my cell and just shakes his head, popping the front of his hat with his thumb. Giving me a scowl like a disappointed parent.

"Thought I wouldn't see back here, Mr. Jackson." Officer Bowers said with a firm low tone.

"And I thought I told you my name is Daniel, not Mr. Jackson." I said with a small huff, "What time did y'all book me in last night?"

Bowers gave a low chuckle, "The boys brought you in at midnight."

"Midnight?" I proclaimed, making my head give a big thump. "Jesus, I must have been way under the table pretty early."

"Yup, talked to your girlfriend last night. She said she would be by to bail you out sometime in the afternoon. Lucky gal you got there, partner"

My head thumped again. I was going to have to spend a whole day behind this cell. And that was *Not* how I wanted to spend my Saturday. But I gotta pay for my idiotic actions so maybe behind bars is a good thing. It'll help me clear my head and try to do things better in the future.

"Lunch is in two hours. Need me to get you some water, Mr.-" Bowers cleared his throat, "Daniel?"

"Yes, please."

Officer Bowers nods his head and walks past my cell. I laid back down and placed my hands over the back of my head. I stared up at the ceiling, thinking, pondering, wishing I could do better.

A few moments later, Bowers comes back with a cup of water. He places it in the slot between the bars and tips his hat. I got up and chugged the water so fast, I would have thought there would be a shortage at some point soon. Before I could tell him thanks the power went out, making the emergency lights flash on.

Bowers's radio walkie-talkie started to go crazy with someone shouting about backup, followed by a few gunfires.

"This Bowers, talk to me," he said into the mic on his shoulder.

"We need all available units to report downtown. Some sort of mass hysteria has taken over the Scarecrow parade. People are attacking others and they will not -" more gunfire ringed out. "Jesus Christ, they're eating them. They're eating- "Another round of gunfire followed by the officer on the radio lets out a blood-curdling scream. Then silence.

My heart was pounding, making my head hurt even worse now. I could see that even Officer Bowers was in complete shock.

Another officer ran into the holding cells with sweat running down his face. He had a beer gut belly that was puffing in and out like he had just run a 5k marathon. His cheeks were flustered up to his shaven head.

"Sir," the officer wheezed, "There's something happening downtown. People are eating others and-"

"I heard what was said!" Bowers exclaimed. "Get all units downtown. Riot gear is a must!"

As Bowers was heading out I cried out to him. "Hey! *Hey,* wait! Wh-who is going to be here to watch me?"

Bowers turns to me, walking backward out of the holding cell, "Ah hell Daniel! You're a grown man, you don't need no babysitter." He walks out the door and is gone.

My anxiety was now going out the roof. I could feel what I had for dinner start to come up as well. I ran over to the toilet and puked everything out. Once I was finished I flushed the toilet and then washed my face over the sink. My head was feeling ten times better, but I still had a small headache. I could still hear the officer in my head saying, *They're eating them.* Who was eating who? Mass hysteria? I sat on the bed for a brief moment before I got back up to my feet and started pacing around my cell. God, what I would do for a cigarette right about now?

An hour passes and still nothing. When it was lunch time that's when I started to become worried. The cell was eerily quiet. Suddenly the door to the holding cells busted wide open. I went up to the bars gripping them tightly with my hands trying to squeeze my head to see who just walked in. It was Bowers. He was holding the side of his neck as blood started squirting out between his fingers. His hat was missing which exposed his dark bald head. My eyes widened as he slowly hobbled his way over to me.

"Oh my god!" I took a step back, "Dear Jesus Christ on a stick, what the hell happened to you?"

Bowers walks over, almost as if he had to think about his next step. He reaches down for his ring of keys with one hand not holding his bloody mess of a neck, trying to remove the key carrier from his belt loop. He struggles trying to get the keys off with blood still draining between his fingers. As he gets to the cell next door to me he finally manages to get the keys off his loop. He takes another step forward before collapsing to the ground as a pool of blood starts to stain the floor around him.

I was in complete shock. *"Help!"* I cried out, "Somebody help! Officer down! Officer down!" I could hear my voice echo throughout the entire jail. And yet I didn't hear any rushing footsteps to see why I was shouting. I cried out again, waiting, nothing. I ran my fingers through my hair as I kept staring at the dead body on the ground. I felt like I was stuck in a nightmare. My body was on fire and the jail cells are usually colder than a penguin's toe. I cried out once more and yet... nothing.

I paced back and forth in my cell. Trying to not go insane. Was this really happening? Or did I die while being blacked out drunk and this is my version of hell? As my mind raced with these thoughts I began to hear something outside of my cell. It was low, but it was now the only sound in the building besides my hard breathing. I ran back to the bars and looked towards where Bowers had come in. But there was no one there.

It turned out to be a soft gurgling sound that was coming from Bowers. I watched as the man I believed to be dead, lying in his blood, started to twitch a little. First, his legs, then his arms, and finally his head lifted about 2 inches off the ground and slammed back down. Bowers made a soft growl as he planted his hands face down to lift himself. As he rose from the ground, he started growling a lot louder this time. When he got to his feet his back was hunched over like an elderly man. His face was smeared with blood that tracked all the way down to his uniform. Underneath the blood, his face looked gray, and his eyes were a buttery yellow.

He snarled, sniffing around the room. Then he locked eyes with me. Quickly (almost instinctively) I backed away from my cell bars as Bowers came charging towards me. He slams face first into the bars knocking him backwards and falls to the floor. He got back up like nothing had happened and came straight up to the bars, trying his best to reach me as his arms flailed around, like trying to shoo away a fly. His nose was broken as it was twisted to the side.

"Bowers," I cried out, backing to the far wall, "What the hell is wrong with you?"

But he didn't answer me. He was still trying to break into my cell while snarling, with drool dripping down his face.

There came a loud *Bang.* Bowers stepped away from my cell and gave an insane person a kind of scream. I put my hands over my ear, dropping to my knees as Bowers was getting ready to lunge forward until three more loud *Bangs* cried out into the holding cell as Bowers was shot three times. *BANG-BANG-BANG!* One in both shoulders and the other two in his midsection. Bowers collapsed to the ground. I walked hesitantly over to the cell bars, not taking my eyes off of Bowers.

When I got to the bars I glanced over and could see another officer with his gun still drawn out and pointing at Bowers. A deputy perhaps but this young man looked like he was fresh out of high school. Short blonde hair, and bright sea blue eyes that looked like there was no soul left behind them. Only this poor scared look in his eyes that he was just trying his very best to keep under control. His hands were covered in fresh blood which dripped slowly onto the ground.

"Please!" I exclaimed, "What's going on out there? You gotta let me out!"

The officer walks over to the cell where Bowers had dropped the key, holstering his gun. He bends over and picks it up then walks over to my cell trying to find the right key.

"I have no idea what the fuck is going on." The deputy said, still shuffling through the keys. "One minute the parade is going swell, next thing I hear is some woman yelling and crying that some man is eating her child. When me and another officer got to them the man had been eating the little boy's neck. That's when the mother tried fighting him off then he pounced right on top of her and took a big bite out of her face. Next thing we know the whole town is eating each other like some sort of fucked up plague buffet."

I couldn't believe what I just heard. None of that makes a lick of sense. I felt like I was going insane and might puke everywhere. Then the officer finally finds the key he has been looking for. He tries to place it into the key slot, yet due to his hand being too bloody it slips out and lands on the ground. When he goes to pick it up his wrist is seized by Bowers. The bastard just doesn't know how to stay dead. Bowers takes a huge bite out of the officer's hand, ripping three of his fingers right off. The officer screams like no other man I have heard scream before. The officer takes his gun out of his holster and shoots Bowers in the head. This time the crazed cop had stopped moving with his eyes blankly staring up at the ceiling. A small hole with smoke where a small piece of Bower's brain should have been came rising out of his skull.

The officer staggers away from the cell, holding his head with both hands. He falls to his knees and begins to throw up some sort of black vile. It reeked worse than a gas station bathroom. Then the officer began to wheeze. His head twitches to the side a few times while making an awful groaning noise. His skin was beginning to lose color as it slowly turned to gray. He looks up at me with the same expression Bowers gave me with eyes full of yellow.

"Oh, you got to be kidding me," I said backing away once more. The officer got to his feet and charged at my cell bars, growling, trying his best to get through the bars and not having any luck.

I looked at the officer's feet and could see the gun still lying next to my cell on the other side. I figured if I could get the gun I could stop this… whatever he is and grab the keys. But this officer was on a mission. And if I can put context clues together, he's after my skin. No worse, he was ravenous for my skin, and what lies underneath my skin. But how was I going to get the gun while he was trying to get to me?

I had an idea. A stupid one, but I didn't have much of a choice. And I didn't think I would be lucky for someone else to come and take care of this problem. Not with how crazy it *must* be outside. There was a brief moment where I thought it would be safer in here than out there. Until I saw Rebecca, my girlfriend, inside of my head. Now I became very concerned about her. So, it's now or never for what I had planned.

I lined up my body with the bars the officer was trying to reach through. I said a little prayer in my head, asking god that if this works and I can get out, I'll drop the drinking and start a clean sober life. I slapped myself in the face a few times, took some quick breaths in, and charged at the crazed officer. When I reached the bar I kicked the officer between the two bars and it landed. The officer went flying backward, tripping over Bowers's body, then fell to the floor, ass first.

I dropped to my knees trying to reach for the gun. The officer, still on the ground, quickly glanced over to me and roared. He started crawling towards me as my fingers were doing their best to grab the gun but had little luck. The officer now crawling over Bowers began to reach out for my hand. He was getting closer and I felt like I was just too far from the gun. I gave myself one good push and my fingers finally got it to scoot closer towards me. I grabbed the gun and quickly retreated away from the cell bars as the officer went face first into where he was trying to take hold of me in the first place. The officer growled and hollered trying to reach me from the other side. I raised the gun towards him, my hands trembling. I closed my eyes. For a brief moment, I saw Rebecca's face and all became calm. I took a deep breath in, aimed, and shot at the officer. Right between his eyes.

The officer lay there as smoke rose off of the fresh new hole planted into his skull. I tossed the gun to the side, got to my feet, and yelled loudly at the dead officer. I wasn't sure if it was from sheer delight that I got him with one shot or maybe it was just me trying not to lose my mind. Either way, the bastard was dead and now on to phase two. I gingerly walked over to the cell bars. I kicked the officer in his head to make sure he wouldn't come back like Bowers did and take a bite out of me. But the officer was indeed dead. I got to my knees now reaching for the keys. I got them and tried every key on the ring until I found the right one. A few moments passed and I finally found the key for my cell. I turned it and opened up my cell. Making this my first, and hopefully last time I would have to break out of jail. Free as a bird out of his cage, now walking out into whatever nightmare lay outside of this building.

I was beginning to walk out and something dawned on me. I went back in and grabbed the gun I used to shoot the crazed officer. I checked to see how many rounds were left only to find there were no more bullets in it.

Thank you, God. No more drinking for this S.O.B.

CRYING IN THE CHAPEL

MAMA AND FATHER HAVE BEEN DEAD for some time now, yet I have seen both of them since I started working here at the church. So it's better now I start writing this rather than never doing so at all. Who I am is of no importance but for now, you may call me Nathan. The Fall time storms were beginning to set in and I was in desperate need of finding somewhere to stay for a few days. You see I'm a drifter, I have been one since I was just about thirteen going on fourteen, after my father was sent off to fight in the war and left me and my poor mama at home, as she got sicker and sicker. Mama had caught leukemia and was gone within a month.

My father died in combat against the Vietnamese and left me as an orphan at the ripe age of eleven. I had no other family here in Texas since we came from where I was conceived in Cleveland, Ohio. The only reason why we came to this hotter than Satan's pits state was that none of our family wanted any part in my parent's marriage being it an interracial one at that.

We packed our bags when I was about seven years old and moved to a small town called Sunset, Texas. Then my daddy got the letter for being drafted into the war. Once Mama died the state of Texas placed me into an orphan home while I waited for some snobby family to come by and pick me out. Since I was already older no family wanted a half-breed adolescent and only wanted a child maybe no older than five years.

I only stayed a year at the orphanage house before I decided to leave on my own and travel around until I found my purpose.. Or some sort of inspiration.

(Or maybe I was just angry at the world and wanted to escape.)

Since I left the orphanage nearly nine years ago, I've been working in every little town I stop in until I make enough to keep moving on. Restaurant busboy, lawn mowing, roofing, painting murals for a school in Navasota (this one I actually enjoyed and got paid exceptionally well), plumbing, a little bit of electrical, and so on and so on.

I made it from Giddings from a small town called Bryan until I wound up hitching a ride in the back of a farmer's truck that was hauling bushels of hay. I told him that I was heading to Austin. The old farmer told me to hop in the back, so I did as I was told and threw my pack which carried a huge thermos filled with water, snacks such as apples, pears, and oranges, and my wallet which carried $159, and the only picture I had of me with my parents when I was just about four years old.

About an hour later we stopped outside of Austin in a small town named Manor. I offered him ten bucks but kindly refused it. He wished me the best and I wish him one as well. I watched him drive off as I turned, walked into this small, blink once and thank you come again you're out of it, town.

I could feel my stomach growing hungry and had worked up a good appetite for something tasty. I began to smell an intoxicating aroma of burgers, fried chicken, and Bar-B-Q. Smoke was coming out of the vent hood and I was immediately attracted to the restaurant with a flashy neon sign that read: Willie's Burgers.

As I walked in, the smell of freshly made burgers along with the scent of cigarettes as smoke made the restaurant look a bit hazy. The eleven people who were eating, conversing with each other, or watching the football game on the television had stopped what they were doing and all stared at me. Even though segregation has been over for years now, there are still times and places I go, and can feel the tight noose around my neck. But whenever I get discouraged, one of the last things my father said to me that I can clearly remember was, "Son, there are evil people out here in this world and you have to be the bigger man in any situation. If a man swings at you, you swing harder, but not unless he or she has truly provoked you. Be the better man. You'll know what I mean when you get older."

And I did know exactly what he meant growing up, having to fight off the white people and hell even my own kind because I was too dark for the whites and too light for the blacks. A true cluster fuck is what I am.

I ignored all the blank and possibly hate filled stares and found a place to sit down. A young white woman, maybe no older than seventeen, walks over to my table with a menu and places it on my table. If it wasn't for the strong odor from the burgers and cigarette smoke this young lady could have suffocated me with how much aqua blue was in her hair. She almost looked like Cindi Lauper if she was just a few years younger, but the name on her dimly fading gold badge read, Kimmy.

"Can I getchu something to drink sugar?" Kimmy asked as she smacked hard on her bubble gum.

"Water, and whatever burger is on today's special will be my order as well. Fries will be fine too."

The young lady cocked her right eyebrow up slowly as if she was trying to process my simple order or thought I wouldn't have the funds to pay for such an order… Whatever that was I ordered. Then she smiled and picked the menu off the table without her taking my eyes off me as she blew a pretty decent-sized bubble with her gum. She inhaled it back in as it made a small popping sound and said, "Coming right out sugar."

As she turned away and began to walk off something dawned on me and I called out her name. She pauses and turns her head first then swings her entire body around and approaches my table once more. Another wave of aqua blue rushed over me as she stood over my table but there was a serious question I needed to ask her.

"Would your manager happen to be in today?"

Kimmy was looking at me with a bewildering look, like she was seeing some sort of incomprehensible illusion. She blinked rapidly three times and finally nodded her head.

"Would it be possible if I could speak to him or her please, ma'am?" Now it was me that was raising an eyebrow. This little gesture I learned from a drunken Irish guy one night in Houston. He told me that if I needed a woman to do a certain task without hesitation, just speak low and give them a look like I want to fuck the shit out of them but remain C.C.C (Cool, calm, and collected).

Kimmy blushed and almost dropped her gum from her mouth as she nodded quickly and turned away to put my order in. As she hung the ticket on a string along with the other tickets waiting for the food to go along with them, Kimmy went into the kitchen and from where I was sitting I could see through the serving hatch as she walked up to a balding fat man and began to talk to him.

I could see she was telling him about my request and as she did she pointed over to where I was sitting. I briefly made eye contact with the fat man and he quickly looked away. He begins to ask her something she didn't know as she throws her hands up and shrugs her shoulders in an *I don't know, beats me* kind of gesture. The fat man sighed, walked out of the kitchen, and headed my way.

Before he got to my table I stood up and extended my arm to shake his hand as I introduced myself. The fat man paused in front of me and looked at my hand with a puzzling expression. As if I had a joke buzzer and was waiting for him to take the bait. But he wiped his hand on his side and shook my hand.

"Leonard Hamilton." The fat man said, "My waitress said you would like to have a word with me." He began to look around his restaurant and I didn't even have to look to feel every pair of eyes staring dead at us.

"Yes sir, I was just curious to know if you had any jobs available at the moment."

He glared at me as he worked his eyes up and down my person and then saw my bag with my belongings and asked, "You a drifter?"

"Yes... Sir, I am." I said with a slight surprise.

"Sorry son, I don't hire temporary workers and especially hippies at that."

"I'm sorry sir, but I'm not a hippy. Hell, I don't even drink or do drugs and my father served in 'Nam. So I would like to believe I'm far from it."

By this time Kimmy had come back with my order and my stomach began to growl. Leonard looked over to Kimmy who was fixated on me once more and had caught her manager's gaze and quickly grew small like a puppy who had just been told they were a bad girl. As she left Lenoard turned back to me and sighed.

"Look, Nathan right? You seem like a good guy. You religious any?"

I started to ponder on this question on how queer it was but quickly went to answer him, "Well, I was brought up Baptist and when I was back in the orphanage in my adolescent days they tried to convert everyone to Roman catholic but recently I've just tried to keep an open mind about stuff like that."

Leonard began to nod his head as his double chin began to move in waves. "Well, you see I ask that because just outside of town is a small, well hell I say small but the mother fucker is actually huge, but there's this church that is always looking for someone to do work for them. Saint Theresa is the name of it. I hear they pay very well too. I heard they start at five bucks but you didn't hear that from me."

I felt so ecstatic by this that I didn't even feel hungry anymore - that was a lie on the fact I stuffed my face with that burger once I got done talking to Leonard- that I quickly shook his hand and thanked him. He gave me directions to the church, which wasn't too far. Just an hour and a half walk from here is what he said, then he wished me the best, hoped I enjoyed my food, and went back into the kitchen.

Once I finished eating, Kimmy brought me the check. I paid it and left Kimmy with a ten-dollar tip. I grabbed my things and began making my way towards the church.

I sat under a tree after walking for about 7 miles and the smell of rain was in the air. I can see the top of the church as the cross stands high and tall. Lightning danced across the now dark violet sky as thunder rang out loudly. I threw my pack over my shoulders and began to sprint to try and avoid the approaching rain hoping it would all work out for me.

Hopefully.

• • •

I was fortunately lucky as it did work out, and I'll tell you how it all went down. When I arrived on the church grounds there was an older man attending to a garden in front of the church. And I do say that Leonard, the restaurant manager was right, the church *was* huge. From the outside, it almost resembled a castle. The grass was a mighty green with leaves in neat little piles. The flower garden was painted with many different plants. A letter board read: **St. Theresa** and **Worship from 8 pm-9 pm every Saturday.**

I found the time and day kind of peculiar for a church to hold service late at night, not to mention on a Saturday at that. But I needed the money to find a place to stay and the closest motel around here was a good two-hour walk.

The man outside took notice of me slowly approaching him and the church. He raised to his feet and stood tall and firm. He was an exceptionally tall man for someone who looked like he could just keel over at any minute.

"Good evening my child." The old man greeted, "I do apologize, but the church is closed for the day. But you may return at nine in the morning for anything you need."

"Oh, I'm not here for the service," I began to take my bag off of my shoulders and watched his eyes follow my pack to the ground then back up to my eyes. "I was told that the church is looking to hire someone to keep up with the place."

His expression lit up with both surprise and a touch of relief. "You were told correctly. We have been looking for a handyman to take care of this old building. The church has been up since 1897 if you can believe that and needs some great attention to it."

It was indeed hard to believe. The church looks like something out of a fantasy novel by Tolkien himself. The old man continued, "It's been kept up with for many many years and our old caretaker, James Tharp, God rest his soul, died on the sixth of June. Since then we've been doing somewhat well since his departure to God's kingdom. My my, where are my manners, Peter Sampson is my name. And you are.."

I extended my hand and introduced myself. He shook my hand and I was shocked at how strong the old timer's grip was. It was like shaking hands with a bodybuilder.

"Come, follow me, Nathan. I'll show you around and don't forget about your things." Peter said, waving his hand towards my pack. I picked up my backpack and followed right behind him.

He opened up both tall doors and I was immediately impressed by how big the church was inside. It made the outside look deceitful as there were about thirty rows of pews and the carpet was a clean dark maroon. There were rows of huge light fixtures that hung below. The windows were plastered with events in the Bible such as Noah on the ark with two of the same kind of animals, David about to take out Goliath, and Jesus walking on water, but the one that struck me as odd and out of place was the one with Able fixing to meet his doom by his brother Cain. The eyes on Able almost looked sinister and not to mention Cain's expression of straight horror was just absolutely bone-chilling. It was something that could scar any child and make them not one to come back. Not to mention the crucified Jesus statue on the wall. He was wearing nothing but a wrap around his crotch and had a puncture wound below his ribs with beads of blood running down his side. And his eyes... His eyes were slightly open and looking up towards the heavens with a look on his face that screamed out, *Why God?*

"Now as I said before, the church was built in 1897 and was ordained by a priest by the name of Thad E. Edmon. The church has been through both World Wars, the depression, and one major tornado storm back in 49' that nearly took the entire roof off the place. Through charity events and having the utmost best congregation we managed to pay for a new and better secured roof. The church is broken up into three sections. Where we're at now is what we call the Chapel. This is where we hold our services, weddings, funerals, the whole nine yards." Peter let out a small chuckle which led to a coughing fit. He took out a small handkerchief from his pocket and coughed into it. Maybe it was just the lighting in the church but I could have sworn I saw a small trace of blood on his handkerchief.

He placed his handkerchief back into his pocket as we reached the front of the Chapel. "Over to your right will lead you to our kitchen and what the young kids call a social lounge where you can sit, talk, and eat amongst yourselves. Past the social lounge will lead you to our classrooms. There are five rooms in total but are usually only used on Saturdays after our evening services."

At that point, I asked him why they held services on Saturday evenings and not Sunday mornings like most churches.

"We're not like most churches." Peter began to say. He looked down at his feet as if he was trying to find his next words. He looked up and held out his hand towards the exit out of the Chapel to our left. "We're a small community and our congregation has dramatically dropped after the events of the Cuban Missile Crisis and continued to drop. Most of our congregation are of the elderly bunch. Some are young people such as yourself but it seems Saturdays work best for everyone so we've been holding our services since 1971."

We walked into an office-like room. The only items occupying this room were a small desk, a filing cabinet, a picture Of Saint Michael the Archangel slaying a man, and a red, yellow, and green poster that read: *I'm not mean, I'm motivated!*

"This is the administration office where we do most of our paperwork, files on the congregation, and where our employees would pick up their checks every Tuesday, but since we haven't had an employee since ol' Mr. Tharp passed on it has been a quiet one I'll tell you what. He was such a great soul. It was really sad that- my my, I'm rambling aren't I? So Nathan I'm assuming you know your way around fixing toilets and tending a garden I assume."

Quite the assumption I presumed but he was not wrong. Toilets I have no problem with and I wouldn't say I have a green thumb but I know my way around a daisy or two. So I told him everything that I knew I could do.

"My my, quite the handyman aren't we." He chuckled again but this time he was clear from another coughing attack. "Well the lord must have sent me an angel because here you are."

I shuddered when he said that, I'm not sure why but something in his voice sounded a bit...

Ominous.

"And judging by your bags you must be a traveler correct?"

First time I've heard anyone use the term *traveler* instead of a drifter.

"You could say that, yes sir. I've just been going around town to town until I finally find somewhere I really like and just settle down there. I've picked up a few skills on the way here and there but nothing has made me stop my journey just yet."

"Well now, you are very special indeed. Well, listen, the starting pay is five dollars an hour and you'll only have to work for at least four to six hours a day. Is that something you think you can handle?"

I agreed.

"Can you lift about fifty-plus pounds?"

I nodded my head and agreed.

"Are you looking for a temporary place to stay?"

I paused before I answered and at first confused and the gears in my head began to turn and I nodded my head to this question.

Peter grinned and flashed his sheet of paper-colored white teeth. He walks over to the filing cabinet and pulls out a piece of paper. He sets it on the desk and pulls out a red pen. He began to scribble on the sheet of paper and quickly turned it over to me.

"If we are all in agreement on your employment then I need your John Hancock right next to the red X."

He handed me the red pen and without hesitation I signed it. He rolls up the piece of paper and places it on the top shelf of the filing cabinet. He walks over to me with his hand out and I firmly shake his hand.

"Nathan, I would like to personally welcome you to the Saint Theresa family and how happy I am to have you aboard."

"Thank you, sir, I appreciate the opportunity."

"The pleasure is all mine. Come now, let me show you to your quarters."

We walked back out to the Chapel as Peter was beginning to give me a list of what tasks I would have to complete.

Nothing too serious that I couldn't handle was what I thought as he made everything sound extremely difficult. I'll give him the benefit of the doubt with him being old and all. But as we were coming up to the other end leading into the kitchen, my peripheral picked up on a figure.

I looked over towards the back of the Chapel and I saw a woman, perhaps around my age, sitting by herself and she appeared to be praying. Her hair was a clean brunette and her skin was as white as snow. She was wearing a red and black dress which exposed her shoulders and a bit of her cleavage. As Peter and I made it to the entry to the kitchen the woman looked up and stared at me. Her eyes looked wide and for some reason seemed to have no life behind them. Just two swollen and shallow eyes, as if she had been crying all day. The woman looks back down and begins to pray once again as we enter the kitchen.

Peter led me out of the kitchen and down a hall that held all five classrooms as he explained earlier. At the end was a sixth room. He takes out a huge ring of keys from the side where he keeps his handkerchief and flips through a variety of keys. Once he found the one he was looking for he unlocked the door and we entered into a small bedroom that could almost be mistaken as a dorm or a motel room. There was a small bed on the left side and a bathroom on the opposite side. In other words, it looked cozy.

"This is where you may reside for the time being. My quarters are back on the other side of the administration office if you should require my assistance for anything. How does it look? Any questions?"

"I couldn't have asked for anything better so I greatly appreciate it. I do have one question though."

"Oh, and what that might be?"

"Who was that girl out there in the back of the Chapel before we went into the kitchen?"

"I'm sorry, a girl you say? In the... Chapel?" Peter looked at me with quiet concern.

"Well yeah, I mean yes sir. She was sitting by herself and possibly praying. She looked really sad as well."

Peter began to open his mouth and made a small grunt. "I'm sorry Nathan but as I said before, we are closed. No one is permitted on church grounds unless premiered otherwise. There was no one in the Chapel I can assure you of."

"Oh," That's all the words I could find. I knew I saw her, I know I did.

Didn't I?

"You're possibly tired, my child. Why don't you get freshened up and I'll cook us some supper before we head off to sleep. We have a big day tomorrow the both of us so we need to be well rested. There are towels in the linen closet as soon as you walk into the bathroom. The supper will be ready in about thirty minutes. If you need anything just holler."

He walked out of the room and gently closed the door behind him. I placed my pack next to the bed and looked around the old room and began to ponder about that woman. I know I saw her, I know I did. I know I did!

Didn't I?

• • •

Later that night I woke up from having an awful nightmare. I was dreaming that I was already working here at the church. I was over in the Chapel vacuuming down the pews when there came a sudden sound of a group of people yelling in unison. I immediately jumped in fear and slowly went to check on where that sound came from. As I entered the kitchen the sound of yelling rose again. When I entered the hallway that led to the classrooms and at the end of the hall near where my sleeping quarters were, there was a crowd of people, almost resembling the people I saw back at Willie's Burgers. There was even the manager, Leonard, who was a part of the crowd. And even, Peter was a part of it.

The crowd was all huddled in a circle and appeared to be looking down (not looking but deeply staring) at something on the ground. I slowly walked closer to the group and I could see someone lying on the ground naked in a fetal position. It was Kimmy, the waitress from Willie's Burgers.

Kimmy lay on the ground holding her knees up to her chest and whimpering. The crowd took in a deep breath all together and gave another loud shot at the girl lying on the floor. Their screams rang loud enough I placed my hands around my ears. It almost sounded worse than someone taking their fingernails and running it across a chalkboard.

Peter, who had his back towards me, stood up straight and began to slowly turn around, along with Leonard and a very tall old woman with black streaks in her bright white hair running down in thin strips. This woman was a mystery to me for I have never seen her before in my life. As they turned to face me, their faces began to melt away and would be replaced by the heads of wild animals. The old woman's face turned into a fox, Leonard's turned into a wolf, and Peter's turned into what looked like a Tasmanian devil. I have never seen a Tasmanian in person, only on wildlife TV shows and whenever Loony Tunes had thrown in that slobbering twister toon in there.

The Tasmanian opened up its mouth wide and out flew three Crows that flew my way and passed over my head. Peter's mouth was still open as it took in a huge breath of air and held it in. In my dream, I could hear it about to scream or yell but as it did there was no audio behind the scream, or anything else going on. Silence had consumed the hall we were in but in my dream, it was like I could still hear the screams from the crowd and the Tasmanian devil as I once more placed my hand over my ears and I shut my eyes tightly.

When I opened my eyes back up, the three that turned to me were gone and now the crowd that was staring at Kimmy, as she still lay on the ground crying, were all staring at me. Their eyes were bigger than normal and there was rage, hate, and resentment in their glare. No one made a sound or moved a muscle. I began to back away as they all began to raise a hand out towards me. That's when I could feel someone's cold hands gently caressing the sides of my neck before they squeezed down hard, nearly puncturing the skin. I tried to scream but as I did I finally awoke from my nightmare.

I sat up quickly as I gasped for air and was swatting at the air like walking into a cloud of gnats. After several seconds of coming back into reality, I sat on my bed ran my hands through my hair, and realized it was only a dream. I took a deep breath in and threw the covers off of me to cool down my sweaty body. After a few more seconds I slowly laid back down threw my hands behind my head and stared up at the ceiling, trying to make myself tired again. I could feel my once pounding and pulsating heart trying to thump out of my chest and come to a steady and calm beat.

As I began to close my eyes I began to hear the sound of someone crying coming from outside of my room. My eyes sprang open as I lay there confused and a little distraught. The crying reminded me of the nightmare I previously had as the sound seemed to be coming from a woman. I swiftly threw my feet onto the ground and sat straight up as I tried to pay attention to the sounds returning in this giant darkened church.

I got to my feet and began to walk towards the door leading out to the hallway. I paused and pressed my ear against the door. The sobs of the woman didn't seem to be coming outside of my room, but it did seem close by. Her sniffles echoed loudly as she continued to cry some more. This time it wasn't my imagination and I was hearing a woman in the church.

I cautiously opened up my door and the bright red digital clock at the end of the hall was my only light source as it read out 3:37 AM. As I walked out of my room the entire church fell silent and the crying had stopped.

I looked around still standing outside of my room to see if there was any sign of life or any other questionable sounds that I would have to discuss with Peter when we got our day started. But there was not a single sound except for the wind blowing extra hard that made a small whistling noise as it brushed against the church. I began to suspect that I was still dreaming until there came a new sound coming from down the hallway that sounded like a whisper.

"We're closer than you think we are." A voice quietly whispered. I stared down the hall to see what or who was speaking softly when a tiny object rolled from out of the kitchen and into the hall. It stopped dead center for a brief moment and continued to roll down the hall and toward me. I could feel my heart racing once more as the tiny ball-like object was getting closer and closer. When the tiny object got

to my feet I slowly bent down to pick it up. As soon as my fingers made contact it felt like it was wet or had been dipped in some sort of oil. I picked up and turned around to the window that the moon was trying to peek through and saw I was holding an eye. I assumed it was an eye but there was something off about the pupils that I wished I would have studied a bit more before throwing it back on the ground in disgust.

The eye dropped to the floor and immediately began to roll away back towards the kitchen again. I followed with my eyes and noticed someone standing at the end of the hall. It was a tall dark cloaked figure just standing there as the eyeball rolled past him and back into the kitchen. The tall dark figure turned and walked into the kitchen.

At that point, I ran back into my room and shut the door as it made a loud bang that carried throughout the church and I was afraid of waking up Peter. I backed away slowly and retreated to my bed.

I stayed up for a few hours watching my door and keeping a keen ear out to hear any other suspicious noises until my eyes grew tired and I finally fell back asleep. I didn't dream again and to be honest, I'm pretty happy I didn't.

• • •

I never did tell Peter about what happened two nights ago on the account that I didn't want him to think I was some druggie or a schizophrenic. I came across this job out of sheer luck (not) and I needed the money. The past two days have not been as bad as I thought it would be. To be frank, I've felt like I've just been inspecting the place for small chips in the paint, dirt on the floor, greasy stove tops, dirty tables, pews, and a few doors.

Easy money.

Peter would later tell me as I helped him out in the garden, he would have a select few from the congregation meet at the church to go over what will be discussed in tomorrow's service. He asked me if I was a religious type and I told him I believed in a higher power, just not maybe the same one that they worshiped, but I've always kept an open mind. He nodded his head slowly and told me that since I was not part of the congregation I was strongly advised to not interrupt their meeting. And it was the way he said it that sounded a bit off. It made me feel like they were holding a meeting with the Legion Of Doom from the DC comics.

I agreed that I would stay in my room while they held their meeting. And after supper, that's what I did. Or at least tried too.

As I lay in my bed hoping to get an early night's rest, I heard my name being softly called outside of my room. The voice sounded oddly familiar. I carefully got out of bed stood as still as possible and listened closely.

"*Naathaan…*" The voice called out.

"Mama?" I said, not even thinking about it. I didn't know if it was my mother or not but I had a strong intuition about knowing what my mother sounds like, and whatever it was outside my room sounded damn near like her.

I walked hastily to my door and quietly opened it. As I did the voice called out to me again as I poked my head out. When I looked down the hall I saw not just my mama but my father as well standing together hand in hand at the end of the hallway. My skin was consumed by goosebumps and I could feel my eyes begin to water.

"Mama..?" I said, trying to fight my tears. I pulled my head back into my room so I could open the door all the way. By the time I walked out into the hall, they were both gone. I began to walk down the hall to maybe let my imagination or whatever I just saw let me see my parents one last time.

"*Thisssss way, Naathaan...*" Mama's voice coming from the kitchen. My hands suddenly became sweaty and shaky. Not sure if it was from being overly excited or just downright scared. I know they're gone but I know I saw them, I know it! As plain as day I did.

When I reached the end of the hall I began to hear other voices echoing throughout the church. They weren't yelling or shouting but enough that I could catch a few words here and there.

(We're closer now)

I stopped at the end of the hall and listened closely. I began to hear Peter say something followed by a loud man with a very deep Southern accent and later would be cut off by a woman. This would go on as I began to approach the kitchen. Once I was in, Momma was standing at the other end of the kitchen completely motionless until she turned her body and went into the Chapel.

A door slammed open followed by Peter proclaiming to keep their voices down. I stopped midway through the kitchen as I was following momma I could hear the sounds of footsteps heading towards the kitchen. At this moment I suddenly remembered I needed to be back in my room not intervening with their meeting.

I ducked behind the island counter and hid there as I heard someone walk in and went straight to the refrigerator. In curiosity, I peeked my head just a bit over the counter and my eyes got wide and my heart began to pound.

155

It was a lady, a tall one at that, wearing a black business suit and pants. She had red high heels on and her hair… Was black with thin white streaks coming down it. She seemed to be wearing some sort of mask on the count that a thin wire strap went around the back of her head.

She grabbed a huge jug of something with a thick red coating on it (*blood, it's blood of the youth*) and as she turned I could see a glimpse of the mask she wore which looked like a fox.

"*Lisssten closely, Naathaan.*" A voice whispered out.

I shuffled to the end of the island counter and peeked my head over to see across the Chapel. The door leading into the administration office was still open and I could hear the continuation of the conversation that was going on.

"Tonight is the night, Peter." The man with the deep accent said.

"I'm fully aware of this." Peter replied, "And all is in place as it should be."

"Oh," The woman with the fox mask said, "We need one more host for the ritual and we already have the girl from that awful restaurant Leonard owns, what's it called again? Willie's? Terrible name for a terrible restaurant."

Ritual? Host? And were they just talking about Leonard and Kimmy? My head was racing and my heart was in the same boat as it sank into my bowls. I wanted to leave but I wanted to hear what exactly was going on.

"Do you have our final host for this evening?" The woman said.

"By the grace of the higher-ups I do. Let me show you." Peter said. There was a slight pause along with the sound of papers being shuffled around. "See, poor sap didn't take time to read it," He begins to chuckle, "He just signed it!" Now Peter has broken into a complete laughing attack.

"Ahhh," The woman said satisfyingly. "And who is this... Nathan?"

At that point, I scurried backward and tried to get to my feet. As I tried to make a break to my room, the woman I saw (I knew it, I saw her! I knew I did!) standing right in front of me with tears running down her cheeks as the mascara she wore made large black streaks. I was stunned, and the expression on her face resembled the same. She stood there with the sniffles and not saying a word.

I put my index finger over my mouth in a shushing manner and began to walk around her. As I did she watched me every step of the way, not taking her eyes off me. When I made it to the hallway a cold rush ran through me

(*They know you know!*)

And I turned back to where the crying woman stood and she was gone. I looked around the kitchen and there was no one to be seen. I shook my head, ran back to my room, and closed the door gently. I looked around my room in fear and confusion.

What the hell is going on here?

And what was I supposed to be hosting?

The sound of thunder roared outside which made me jump a little. I wanted to pack up all my things and just get out of here but the sudden storm said otherwise.

As I went to sit on my bed there came a rapping on my door. I stood straight up. My heart pounding and ready to escape out of my chest. I stood by my bed until another rapping came once more. I walked up to it, opened it, and saw no one there. I looked outside of my room to find no one in the hallway as well.

That was until someone stepped into the hallway wearing a Ravens mask along with a suit, a dark red tie, and black slacks.

"Is that him?" The man in the Ravens mask said as he pointed my way.

I immediately closed my door and pushed my bed in front of it. As I backed away from the barricaded door I could hear the sound of a long scratchy rasp. I slowly turned and it was the woman who had been crying in the red dress standing right behind me with her eyes rolled to the back of her head. The whites of her eyes were the window into her empty soul as her jaw hung unhinged and crooked. She continued to inhale slowly as blood began to run down her tear ducts, her jaw made a painful crack as it adjusted itself back in place and she screamed,

"*!!Ruuuuunnnnn!!*"

I nearly jumped out of my skin as I ran to my door and moved the bed out of the way. As I busted through the door, the man wearing the Ravens mask just so happened to be standing behind it and I knocked him clean out as I came out. The raven-masked man fell to the floor with a hard thump as I stepped out of my room. I hurdled over his body and ran down the hall.

Thunder once again boomed loudly outside as I reached the end of the hall. A rather large man who was wearing a wolf mask stood between the exit of the kitchen leading into the Chapel. His back was faced towards me as I cautiously entered the kitchen.

I checked behind me to make sure the man I ran into was still unconscious only to find the crying woman had picked him up by his head. She held the man's face above her head and the man tried to break her grip but was having no luck. The woman bends her neck backwards making loud cracking noises. That's when the man she was holding fell numb as his skull began to enclave on itself before the sound of bone being crushed and cracking. Blood and brain matter spilled over the woman's hand.

As I looked away and back into the kitchen the man in the wolf mask was towering over me. I was paralyzed by the fact that I knew who this man was.

It was Leonard the restaurant manager.

"Going so soon, you dirty hippy," Leonard said.

At that moment I punched him as hard as I could in his fat throat as he grabbed at it with lost air, wheezing, and dropped down to one knee. I pushed him over to the side and made a break for the Chapel.

The entire room that was the Chapel had been filled with over twenty people, all wearing different types of animal and bird masks and... They all had a handful of people's heads. Women, men, black, white, Hispanic, and I believed I saw the head of a child that a woman with a Storks mask was holding.

I even saw the head of Kimmy in a tall man's hand.

"Oh, my dear child," Peter said, stepping out of the crowd and removing his Tasmanian mask. "You weren't supposed to find out this way."

"What the *Hell* is going on here." I proclaimed.

Peter clicks his tongue in a dissatisfying tone. "Now, now, there's no need to curse while in a church."

"Screw you and whatever this is! Telling me not to curse!? You all have severed heads in your hands and you're telling me not to-"

"Enough!" Lenaord roared as he crept up behind me. He swung a fist across the back of my head and I fell face first into the carpet.

There came a sudden pressure over my body like gravity was weighing me down. I couldn't get up. The crowd of people that occupied the Chapel all started to carefully crowd over me and began to softly hum. As the gaps closed in around me I still was having trouble lifting myself back up. Then... That's when the shouting started.

All in unison they took a deep breath in and shouted. It was like thousands of tiny needles being pierced into my body. "Why... Are you doing this...?" I barely managed to say.

The people in the masks all started to hum and I saw a pair of dark shoes that glistened from the chandelier lights above me. Then Peter bent down over me with a paper in his hand. He placed the paper in front of my face and I started to feel cold. It read:

This document is intended for the members of Thad. E Edmon's Cult. To whom signs this document shall have three spirits visit him or her before The Sanction Ritual can commence. Once he or she has seen all three spirits the new host shall be appointed or shall be greatly sacrificed to the Death Demon. As of September 29th, 1981 the applicant signing has agreed to sell his or her soul over to the cult. Long live Thad E. Edmon aka Death Demon.

And under that was my signature.

"Now tell me, my child," Peter began to say. "Which spirits have you come across?"

The crowd around me gave another shout and the feeling of needles grew stronger around my body.

"Up... Yours... You bastard." I replied with the feeling of an elephant sitting on my chest.

"Come on, let's just cut his head off already!" Lenaord said.

"*No!*" Peter snapped. "You know he must confess about the spirits he saw as part of the ritual! Now speak!"

The next wave of shouts from the crowd around me felt as if something inside of my stomach was trying to burst out. I tried lifting my head but I was still unable to. The crowd began to hum softly again

I screamed and Peter said, "The pain will only continue until you tell us-"

"My parents!" I finally confessed. "My momma and father! And... A woman... A crying woman!"

All at once the crowd went quiet, and Peter slowly stood straight up making the joints in his knees pop. The crowd began to murmur amongst themselves and they seemed to be concerned about something. I had a strong feeling it was something I just said.

Lenaord quickly walked over to Peter and I could hear him tell him, "She's back, that harlot spirit will ruin everything again! I told you let's just cut his head off and get it over with."

"You must have a death wish if you are so anal about going against the master's instructions." Peter sharply whispered.

"We need one more soul for the ritual and this po boy bastard just happened to walk right into our grasp. Don't you want to live forever? Don't you know we're running out of time?! I can see it already, you're withering away. Coughing up blood as well, I assume."

Peter turned and I could see his feet pointed towards me as he let out a sigh. "You're right. We have a few more hours left. Give me your cleaver."

I could feel my heart ready to leap out of my chest as tears now began to roll down my face. "Wait, please wait. Don't do this! You ain't gotta do this, please!"

"I'm deeply sorry, my child," Peter said as he bent down to get eye level with me once more. "But without the twenty-three sacrifices, we can't keep living like we have for the past two hundred and sixty-five years. What you're doing is for the best of keeping a legacy alive! Please understand that. It'll only hurt for a bit and then all will be bliss." Peter stands back up and tells the crowd for five more shouts.

The crowd shouts, sending a wave of heat like standing in front of a burning building washed over me; then I began to feel cold as if diving into the Frio river on a winter's day all at once. They shouted again and this time the feeling of thousands of tiny needles crept up from the tips of my toenails to the top of my scalp. I could hear Peter begin to hum as the crowd gave a third shout.

The lights above flickered for a brief moment and immediately went dark. Then there came the sound of a woman crying that started to grow louder and louder.

"Christ, she's already here," Lenaord said. "We gotta hurry!"

The crowd gave a fourth loud shout and then a woman in the back of the crowd began to scream in agony. The feeling in my arms began to come back to life as I was able to move them. Everyone in the crowd ahead of me began to split into two sides and I could see the woman that had screamed. It was the tall old lady who wore a fox mask being lifted into the air by some unknown force. Her mask slipped off of her head as her mouth began to spread open and the top of her head split in two as blood squirted out of her throat. Her lifeless body fell to the floor with a loud thump.

"No," Lenaord pleaded. "No, no God dammit we were so close!"

At that moment, whatever spell they had over me broke and I was able to move again. I scrambled to my feet and came eye to eye with Peter. Peter brings the cleaver up and swings at me. I put my hands up and the cleaver came into contact with both my hands, slashing but not too deep. Peter brings the cleaver around again aiming for my midsection but I carefully dodged it and saw my opening. I swung my fist as hard as I could and came into contact with his jaw.

Peter falls backward and drops the cleaver. Another person in the crowd was suspended into the air by the unknown force (assuming it was the crying woman) this time being a man who wore a bear mask as he screamed and pleaded for someone to help him. But it was too late as his eyes burst out from his skull and he dropped to the ground dead.

I looked down and saw the knife lying next to Peter's unconscious body. As I looked back up I could see Lenaord looking right at the knife then turned his attention to me. Both he and I dove to the ground after the cleaver and I was the one to put my hands over it first.

Leonard punched me in my face, causing everything to go hazy and my ears began to ring. But I held on to the cleaver and quickly rolled over to my back to get back on to my feet. When I was finally back up I turned to face Leonard who was already back up as well and started to charge towards me. I stuck the cleaver out without even knowing I already had. I shut my eyes tightly and felt Lenaord's midsection strike the cleaver as my arm jerked backward.

I opened my eyes and saw Lenaord with a bewildered look on his face. We both looked down together and saw his blood run down the cleaver and dripped onto the carpet floor. He takes his hands and places them over mine, yanking the cleaver out of his fat stomach, and starts to cough blood. Leonard staggers backward before his eyes roll to the back of his head and he falls backward next to Peter's body and dies right there.

The crowd of people was still screaming and being hoisted into the air before they suffered and dropped to the floor dead. I frantically looked around as I felt I was going insane. Finally, at the end of the Chapel, I saw them once more.

Mama and Father were standing next to the exit as the doors swung open.

"Run baby," Mama said.

"Get out of here boy," Father said. "Quickly now!

I didn't argue as I hurtled my way over the dead cult member's bodies and ran up to my parents. Both of them smiled at me and I started to cry.

Suddenly a large roar came from the front of the church that boomed loud enough and made some of the hanging lights fall straight to the ground. Standing straight down the aisle looking dead at me was the tall hooded figure I saw earlier. It was a man whose face was deathly gray and had long snowy white hair. His eyes shined brightly red as he lifted his arm and pointed to me with very long yellow nails.

"His soul belongs to me!" The gray man growled. He began to hover his way over the dead bodies and I could feel him trying to pull me to him.

Both Mama and Father stepped out in front of me as the force that was pulling me had gone away.

"Get out of here Nathan! We love you so much!" Mama exclaimed.

"We got it from here. Go. Now!" Father said.

I wiped my tears from my face, turned, and ran out of the church.

"No!" The gray man bellowed. I turned to look back at my parents one last time they were both staring back at me. The gray man came up behind them and grew exceptionally

large. The crying woman appeared right behind my parents before the gray man could touch them. I could hear my father and mama say goodbye as the doors to church slammed closed.

All the commotion that was coming from inside the church had gone away like hearing a white noise for so long and it just went away. I stood out in the rain as I looked up into the sky and let the cool rain splash my face.

The church suddenly bursts into flames and starts to crumble away. A piece of burning parchment shot out of the church and floated its way to me. I reached up and saw it was the document I had signed when I first arrived at the church. As I held it in my hands it slowly turned to dust then to clumps of mud due to the rain.

A few days later I went back, after coming up with a few dollars until I could get back what I lost from the church fire, and found myself heading back to the orphanage. The older black lady who was a receptionist when I first arrived as an adolescent hollered in joy when she saw who I was. She came around her desk and came up to me with a big ol hug. I told her my adventures since I left the orphanage (minus the whole church business). I would come to ask her about a possible job opportunity to teach the kids about housing maintenance. She flashed a huge smile and said she would talk about it with her boss but to keep a positive attitude.

Her face lit up as something dawned on her. "The strange just keeps getting stranger, I'll tell you what. This came in the mail a few days ago addressed to you. We were gonna throw it away but something told me to hold on to it for you."

I took the letter, opened it up, and read it.

Nathan, I don't know if this will ever reach you but just know we will always be closer than you think. Never give up on being who you want to be. Mama and father love you so much and your guardian angel will also always watch over you. Stay strong…

There was no mention of who this letter was from but I had a strong feeling I knew who it was. Even in the afterlife, I know my parents are still watching over me. And it's crazy to think that Mama and Father, who's been dead for years now, would have saved my life. And also the spirit of a woman who was crying in the chapel.

PEAK INSANITY

BEFORE I GO COMPLETELY MAD I want to tell my side of the story. I feel my mind fading into an everlasting darkness but I wanted someone to hear my story on what happened on September 12th of this year. The day I lost everything and everyone. The day that drew me to the brink of insanity. My name is Kane T. Austin and this is what happened in a small community in Texas.

Before we start I have to talk about what happened a week before shit had hit the fan. I was in the hospital taking care of my wife Elizabeth. We were married for sixteen years and a few months ago she was diagnosed with a brain tumor. The doctor said it was the size of a golf ball. They gave her four months to live. Well, she made it in five months. And on her last day, she was sleeping soundly on her bed. I was watching the Cowboys lose against the Jaguars. There was rain starting to pour down and the room was dark with only the emergency lights on.

All in an instant Elizabeth started to toss and turn in bed, her heart monitor was beginning to pick up speed. She started to hyperventilate as I got to my feet. When I tried to wake her she sat straight up and screamed like she had just seen a ghost. She stopped screaming to say, "It's here." Elizabeth laid back down as her eyes rolled to the back of her head and was dead before the nurses made it to her room. When they came in I was bawling my eyes out over my now dead wife.

A week later I was still adjusting to living in my big house by myself. It was quiet. Well I take it back, we lived in a small community of only sixty-seven people here in Hershel, Texas. I was the only one in town that lived on a farm with my closest neighbors being a good ten-minute walk. Everyone had a car but since everything was close by, (store, pharmacy, bank,) we all just got around on foot.

I had to run by the store to pick up what I was going to be making for dinner for the week. It was hard eating by myself, no one to talk about how the day was, or did you hear about such and such, or just hearing her say I love you. On my walk back home I stumbled across a black cat. Elizabeth always loved cats but she had a specific love for black cats.

"People usually see them as unlucky," Elizabeth used to say, "but to me, I think they are beautiful."

But this cat seemed a bit ominous to me. It just kept staring at me and sitting as still as a statue. If it wasn't for it blinking and moving its body up and down as it breathed I would have honestly thought that cat was some sort of lawn ornament like a grass gnome. As I passed it, the cat just kept staring at me. When it finally moved it poked its head upwards and stared at the sky.

Just like the cat, I too was curious to see what caught its attention. Above us were dark clouds as if it was about to rain. The air became cooler and gave me a small chill. And for a brief second, I saw something move in the clouds. It wasn't a plane or a bird, but it was huge. I kept staring until I could see it again, but nothing ever appeared. I shook my head and thought it was just my imagination. I wasn't able to get much sleep after Elizabeth died and I just blamed it on being exhausted.

When I looked back down to see what the cat would be looking at next it was gone. I searched for it like it was my keys to my car and I was running late for whatever reason I needed to drive and had no luck. I shrugged and continued heading back home.

A storm finally came through as I was getting dinner ready. The rain rapped on the roof of my house. When I looked out the kitchen window I couldn't see ten feet ahead of me. It was coming down that hard. Lightning crashed and thunder boomed. I finished making my dinner and sat down in the den to watch some TV. Elizabeth always liked watching Family Feud and that's what I ended up watching most evenings. I always fancied Steve Harvey and the suits he would wear. Elizabeth told me I would look sexy if I dressed like him. God how I just miss our conversations.

Thunder wailed and the power went out. I cursed into the air as I got out of my chair. I took my dishes back to the kitchen and let them soak in the sink. As I walked over to the window to check on the storm it was still raining cats and dogs. In an instant, it stopped raining. Like as if someone had hit the 'off' button. I got goosebumps all over my body. In my thirty-plus years of existence, I have never seen rain come to a complete halt.

I went outside and looked at the sky above. The clouds were still a dark gray and they seemed to be moving fast. Lightning danced behind the clouds. Just up ahead a funnel started to take form in the sky. I thought a tornado would be touching down soon but something else happened. The funnel spun downwards and stopped. There was an orange light rapidly blinking in the clouds as it traversed towards the funnel. It hovered at the very top before whatever it was shot straight into the ground. The funnel then started to ascend back into the clouds before it went away completely. Then the rain started to pour down once more.

***

I ran back inside to grab my raincoat and car keys. I drove to where I believed whatever came out of the sky had landed and I could see someone else had the same idea. Hal Shofter, owner of Hal's BBQ. Hal was also a long-time friend of mine. He was there for me when I needed a shoulder to cry on at Elizabeth's funeral. He's the only man in Hershel that drives a Chevy pickup in a Ford Nation not to mention him and I are the only black men in town. His huge muscular body nearly stood out in the rain as he turned and waved at me.

As I pulled up behind his truck another car pulled in behind us. Linda Douglas who teaches kindergarten in Navasota. Great gal. A really good-looking gal at that too. Always ready to lend a hand whenever someone needed it. She got out of her car, opened up an umbrella, and met us in the middle next to my car.

"Did you see the rain stop?" Linda said, nearly shouting over the beating rain as she pushed her blonde hair out of her face.

"Yup," Hal nodded, "darndest thing I've ever seen."

"There was something in the sky," I said, trying to get a look at what came out of the sky. Hal and Linda both turned to look at me with puzzlement.

"Like a plane or..?" Linda asked.

"I don't know, but whatever it was I think it landed over there."

"Well let's take a look. My knickers are getting wet." Hal said as he started to walk towards the crash site. Linda and I followed right behind him.

As we got closer there started to be a faint smell. It was like burning rubber mixed with some vile mixture of death and shit. God, I can still smell that odor to this very day. We looked around until Linda pointed out a huge crater. Getting closer to the crash site there started to be a faint hum in the air. I thought I was the only one to hear it but seeing Hal mess with his ears like trying to get them to pop after being at a high altitude. Linda also tried covering one ear while trying to keep the umbrella over her.

"Y'all hear that too right?" I asked. I didn't know if I was shouting but it was loud enough for both of them as they gave me a nod in confirmation. The land we were on was what separated my land and my neighbors Sonny and Vivian Easton.

We approached the crash site and looked inside. It was something that we should have never messed with. It looked to be some sort of slab or tablet. It was small and rectangular. Perhaps about fifteen inches long. The color was something I speculated over. It was like a transparent metallic color. Also, it seemed to have been reflecting some sort of light when there was no light at all. Just the pouring rain and the lightning that flashed the sky.

I bent over to get a better look. As I did Linda placed a hand over my shoulder. I thought she was going to advise me not to get any closer. Only that's not what she wanted my attention for. I looked at her and she shifted her head upwards staring straight ahead. I looked and it was Sonny and Vivian driving up in their golf cart.

They stopped right in front of the crater as they both got out. The suspensions gave a loud clang on their golf cart as both of them were a heavy-set couple. Vivian had a matching yellow raincoat and boots as she opened up her umbrella. Sonny had a raincoat and hat as the water would trickle down to his big gut.

"Kane, Hal, Linda." Sonny nods to all of us. His way of saying hello. We all nodded back at him. "What we got here?

Y'all see how that rain stopped like that there?" Only that last part came out *Dat Derr*.

"Yup," Hal said. "Kane here said he saw something in the sky."

Vivian's eyes lit up, "Like a UFO?"

"I wouldn't say that," I said, still fixated on the small slab. The humming was still there and I could have sworn I heard it... talking. "But whatever it was, it dropped this thing here before taking off again."

"Did you get a good look at it?" Sonny said, trying to bend down to inspect the slab with me and having some trouble doing so. The man was pushing sixty but he got down just the same.

"I didn't. The clouds were still too thick to see anything."

Sonny started to reach for the slab to pick it up. Before he did Vivian placed her hand on his shoulder just as Linda did with me, only this time Vivian would be the one to advise not touching this weird object that fell from the sky. And I wished we had listened to her.

"Can't know what it is if we don't get a better look," Sonny said, now reaching for it once more. He picks up the slab and puts it close to his face. When he did there seemed to be some sort of small sliver of illuminating white light. He stared at it for a good while, almost in a trance-like state. He turns it over and then back again. Hal stuck out his hand to be the next person to inspect it. But it was like Sonny wasn't even here anymore. I almost believed he was about to eat the damn thing.

"Sonny?" Hal said softly. But to Sonny, it was as if he shouted at him as he gave a small jump and noticed Hal's outstretched hand. "Everything alright?"

"Fine, fine," Sonny licked his lips and grunted standing back up before handing over the slab to Hal.

Hal took the slab. He bounced it with both hands in a hot potato way. Then he tossed it over to me with a small huff. I caught it expecting to have my hands burning as well but there was no heat coming from it. Honestly, it felt light and there was a certain feeling to it. A small vibration that made my hands feel tingly. Like if you sat on your hands for too long making them fall asleep. And there was something else that made my hair stand on ends. Images flashed in my head that were too quick to see what exactly it was. The only image I did see was someone standing with their back facing towards me. After that, I started to feel light-headed. I held it out for whoever wanted to inspect it next. And when it was Linda who took it from me, the feeling of being lightheaded was gone. I could still feel the vibrations in my hands as they grew colder.

"My hands are burning," Hal exclaimed. "What the hell is that thing."

"Funny," Linda examines the slab with childlike curiosity. "It's not burning my hands and it seemed it didn't burn Sonny's or Kane's hands. But I do feel... something. I can't explain it but it feels like.." Linda's nose begins to bleed. She was stuck staring at the slab for quite some time before Vivian asked if she was alright. Linda was transfixed on the slab until she dropped it on the ground, stared straight up, and started heading back to her car.

"Linda?" I said with concern, "What's wrong?"

But she kept on walking.

"I'll go check on her," Hal said before taking off running to catch up to Linda.

"We should be going too," Vivian said, worried some. "Right, hon?"

Sonny kept staring at the slab on the ground and then shook his head. "Right, what should we do with... that?" He pointed to the slab.

"I'll take it with me," I bent over to pick up the slab, feeling the soft vibration in my hand once more. "I'll see if I can find anything on the internet about this. Are you two going to be okay getting back?"

"We'll be fine." Sonny said, now taking his wife's hand, "Make sure ol Linda is doing fine."

"Sure will."

"Let us know about her condition," Vivian shouted heading back to the cart, "And what you find on the internet."

I gave them a thumbs up as I watched them back up and drove off back towards their home.

I turned to see if Hal had caught up to Linda but I could see her car backing up in a hurry, making her tires squeal as she took off down the road until I couldn't see her tail lights anymore. I looked at the slab in my hand. The smell of burning rubber was gone and I didn't feel lightheaded this time.

What I did feel was something watching me. I look over to see Sonny and Vivian's golf cart go into the garage as the door behind them closes. Before I looked back towards mine and Hal's vehicles I saw that black cat again. Sitting in the field getting wet as its fur was drenched. And yet the cat seemed to be unfazed by getting wet. I could feel its bright yellow eyes piercing into me. I watch the cat watching me.

Hal blew on his horn a few times, breaking my gaze with the cat. I looked back and could see him waving at me to get a move on. I looked back towards where the cat had been sitting only to find it gone once more. I searched all around not finding it as I did before early that day. Thunder cracked the sky above. I looked up to the sky as the vibrations from the slab started to pick up. I look back at the slab proceeding my way back to my car.

After that day, my whole world took a turn for the worse. God I wished we had listened to Vivian. But as they say, curiosity killed the cat.

***

Before I headed back home, Hal informed me about how strange Linda acted before taking off. He said her eyes seemed almost lifeless. She never responded to him but he explained the odd things she was saying before she got into her car.

"She might have been saying it after she got into her car as well," Hal said. There was fear in his face that I didn't notice until later on. He lost a bit of color as well. "Something about the stars are falling. Know anything about that?"

I shook my head. Then he looked down at the slab in my hand.

"What did you plan on doing with that?"

"Don't know yet. I was going to do some research and see if anything about this comes up."

"And if nothing comes up?"

"It's the internet, Hal. Everything is on the internet."

Hal nodded and then rubbed the bridge of his nose with his thumb and index fingers then told me that he was heading home. I told him the same and that would be the last time I saw him. Except for when I showed up to his restaurant the next day. I know that wasn't him, but I'll get to that later.

I got back home, went straight to the den, and sat the slab on the table. I tried the lights but the power was still out. So instead I went into the kitchen, shuffled through one of the kitchen drawers, and got my flashlight. I ran upstairs and grabbed some scented candles I'd never used in the past three years I've had them. They were a Christmas gift from the in-laws. I thought I got it because for some reason I always stink worse than a skunk in the summertime to my mother-in-law. I ran back downstairs and lit the candles. The smell of vanilla ice cream swam up my nostrils as the light of the flames danced on the walls. And not to mention giving the slab a whole new color.

It was no longer a metallic shade but now it was completely black. There were also white specks coming out in tiny dots all around it. Over on the counter in the kitchen sat my laptop which I brought over, sat on the other end of the slab at the dens table, and tried looking this thing up.

No results were found. Not a single one.

When I closed my laptop I immediately noticed the flame on the candle was being attracted to the slab. My eyes widened and I could feel my heart ready to bust out of my chest. Quick images of red, yellow, green, and purple flashed in my head, and that same person with their back facing towards me appeared. My head was light as a cloud.

I shook my head, but that only seemed to have made it worse. When I looked back at the candle the flames were leaning and leaving a dark black dot stain on the candle holder. I blinked once and when I did it again I found myself standing at the other end of the table looking down at the slab. I shivered. I didn't know how I just went from sitting to all of a sudden standing on the opposite end of the table. But I felt... I guess drunk is the best word. But something gravitated me to this unknown slab.

I picked it up, immediately feeling the low vibrations on it. I drew it closer to the candle, watching the flame back away, and then grew larger when I had it damn near touching it. I pulled it back away and the flames grew dim, following the slab as it pulled towards it until the candle flame went out completely.

In the darkness, I saw two(??) bright glowing yellow eyes sitting on top of the opposite end of the table. I shook my head and there was nothing there anymore. I sat the slab back on the table as if it was burning me. I listened as the rain continued to pour down like when Noah built the Ark. I felt drowsy and wasn't sure why. I think I had an idea but this has just been one hell of a day.

I took one last look at the slab before heading upstairs. I thought about taking it up with me but then I decided not to. When I made it to my bedroom I got undressed, laid down on my bed and was immediately asleep. I dreamed horrible things that night and it would only get worse from then on.

***

In my dreams, I was surrounded by darkness and voices all around me. Although these voices weren't exactly English, I started to believe it wasn't even human. It sounded like a bunch of gibberish in a robotic-like tone. A bright light started to immense in front of me. My legs started walking towards it and as I got closer I could hear someone screaming.

Not just someone. It was Elizabeth. The same scream I heard back before she died in the hospital. I could hear her words echoing in my head.

"It's here... it's here... it's..."

When she stopped speaking everything grew quiet. I walked into the light and found myself being lifted high off the ground. The light flashed brightly causing me to shield my eyes. When I opened them back up I was floating in space. I looked below me and could see the earth. Only it wasn't the same blue and green planet you saw on the internet or in movies and TV shows. The world looked like it was on fire. These objects were zooming all around the world in quick long orange flashes.

I glanced upwards and saw the person who kept appearing in those images. My brain flashed when I held the slab. The person was Elizabeth. Even with her back facing towards me I knew it was her. I tried yelling out her name but being in space sound cannot travel. I tried floating closer to her. As I did I noticed her arms were bent in a way as she was holding something in front of her. She whispered in my head, "Don't look. The stars are falling."

Elizabeth slowly starts to turn towards me. The stars in the sky started going out, falling. Heading towards earth. I watched as they crashed making the earth shine bright with fire and flames from where the stars had struck. I noticed a giant ball of flame coming right toward Elizabeth and I.

"Don't look at the ***. The stars are falling, the stars are falling, *THE STARS ARE FALLING, THE STARS ARE FALLING.*"

Before I could see her face I woke up screaming and sweating. My bed is damp from my perspiration. I looked around my room, almost forgetting where I was. I rubbed my face, whipping away the sweat from my forehead. I threw my feet over my bed, sitting there trying to remember my nightmare as the sun beamed heavily into my room. Even though I didn't want to.

"She said," I licked my lips and cleared my throat, "Don't look at the... what?" I got a cold chill when I heard Elizabeth's voice swimming in my head about stars falling and remembering Hal said he heard Linda repeating that after she held the -

My eyes widened. I quickly jumped out of the bed and ran downstairs. I went into the den to find the slab still where I had left it last night. There was a quiet and low hum coming from the slab. I tried the lights for the den and finally, the power was back on. The slab was back to its metallic color again.

There came another sound. This time from the kitchen. I followed the sound and found out it was my cell phone. I went up to it to see it was Hal calling me. I picked it up and hesitated before answering it. I knew deep down inside that something was wrong. Terribly wrong.

I answered it and I could hear Hal breathing heavily, making me worry even more. "Kane? Thank god."

"Hal everything alright?"

"No," he said quickly which made my heart sink. "You said you record Good Morning America on your TV right?"

Good Morning America? I checked my phone for the time to realize it was already ten in the morning. I've never slept that long before. Except for the nights, I would drink myself under the table right after Elizabeth died. I was always an early bird gets the worm kind of guy.

"Kane, you still there?"

"I'm here, Hal. And yeah I do record it so I can watch it and skip the commercials. Why what's going on?"

"I think you should watch it yourself."

"Okay, any word from Linda?" I asked walking to the living room and turning the television on.

"Not a single word. I'm starting to get worried. Vivian called me too. She told me Sonny has some sort of flu or something. The guy is very sick. Vivian was crying her eyes out telling me this."

I flipped through my recorded shows and found a GMA recording from this morning. When I played it Robin Roberts and George Stephanopoulos were sitting close together with faces that seemed more frightened than I have ever seen a news reporter look. They spoke of weird flying objects from all around the world, dropping off some sort of stone tablets from the sky. There were video recordings of things in the sky. People cry out that it's an alien, or god dropping the eleventh commandment, and that the stars are falling. The hosts of GMA were back again and this time explaining that the people that have come in contact with these tablets have been reported either killing people, killing themselves, or even disappearing. Before they cut to the commercial George Stephanopoulos advised everyone if they had seen these tablets, showing a variety of slabs that looked similar to the one on my den table, to stay away from them and not to touch them.

My heart raced. My mind was filled with questions. I put the phone back to my face and asked if Hal was still there. He wasn't. I tried calling him back but it just went straight to voicemail. I shot straight out of my chair and stood there trying to come up with some sort of plan. A plan for what? I wasn't sure. But with Linda MIA, Sonny sick, and now Hal not returning my calls I couldn't sit by with what I have just learned.

I went back into the den to find the slab was now a bright neon purple. It was glowing. Going from really bright to dim. It reminded me of something that was charging like a laptop. Without thinking I raised my hand towards it. The light was growing brighter as I got closer to it.

Don't look at the ***, Elizabeth's voice rang out in my head.

I quickly retracted my arm away from the slab and went back to glowing bright and dim again. I shook my head and headed upstairs to get dressed.

When I left the house I went straight to Easton's residence. Pulling up to their driveway with the car still running I walked up to their door and knocked on it pretty hard as I knew both of them were hard of hearing. I waited and no one came to the door. I knocked again and waited, but still no answer. Trying to not overthink things I walked around to see if I could see them through the windows but all the shades were pulled down. Figuring that Vivian might have run to the store to grab something for Sonny. I went back into my car and tried calling Hal once more. Only to have my call go straight to voicemail with no ringing in between.

I tried Linda's phone but remembered it was a school day, meaning she wouldn't look at her phone until lunch time which was still two hours away. So instead I called up the elementary school she works at in Navasota.

"Sul Ross Elementary," the school secretary said, "This Anna speaking, how may I help you."

"Hi Anna," I said, trying not to sound worried. "Would it be possible for me to speak to Linda Douglas, please? It's an emergency.

"I'm sorry sir but Linda didn't make it in today." She paused. "In fact, we haven't heard from her all morning. Is everything alri-." I hung up before she could finish her question. Because I knew everything was not alright.

And it was only going to get worse.

***

I planned to drive over to Linda's to check up on her first then go over into town to Hal's restaurant. Until that is, I started to get a call on my cell phone. The caller id came up as Hal. When I answered it was not Hal, but his wife Cheriese.

"Kane?" Cheriese cried. Her voice was cracking. She also sounded like she was hyperventilating as well. "Please.. please get to our restaurant. Something is very wrong with... HEY! No! Put that down!" Pans crashed as they made a loud clang on the other end of the phone along with something that sprayed everywhere, making Cheriese and others start coughing. Then the line was disconnected.

So, new plan. I came to a stop at the sign. Instead of turning left to Linda's, I went right, straight into town. As I pulled up to the restaurant I saw glass in one of the windows shattered everywhere outside. People were standing outside, watching all of the commotion going on inside with Cheriese calling for her husband to come out while some others were recording on their phones. I pushed my way past the crowd and went in.

There was some sort of foam that I had assumed to be from a fire extinguisher, although I never smelt anything burning. Tables and chairs were flipped around and scattered everywhere. I even saw a few traces of blood. I found Cheriese in the back of the kitchen. She gasped as I approached her as if I was some sort of monster.

"What's wrong?" I frantically asked. "Where is Hal?"

Cheriese sniffled, "He's in there." She pointed to a supply closet. "After he got off the phone with you he just started acting funny. He never blinked. He looked brainless. He went all around the restaurant saying that the stars were falling and it's here, it's here. Then he took all the fire extinguishers and emptied them all. Mr Dickery, the pharmacist, tried to talk to Hal, to get him to calm down. But when he tried to take the fire extinguisher away, Hal smacked him in the face with it. Knocking out almost his entire teeth. Then... then..." She turned to look at the door as tears streamed down her cheeks. There was shuffling going on and things being knocked around on the other side of the supply closet door. "Then he just started hollering. The most awful scream I have ever heard a man produce. I tried to get him to stop but he pushed me to the ground, picked up a chair, and tossed it out the window. He kept hollering, Kane, until he ran back here and locked himself in." Now she couldn't stop crying as her breathing became rapid.

I reached out to hold her shoulder and tell her everything was going to be alright. But before I could even touch her Hal opened the door in a quick hurry. He was covered in cooking oil from head to foot. He stared at us like a coyote with rabies.

"It's here," Hal whispered. "We're too late. It's here. It's here. It's here."

"Hal, listen to me." I took a step forward, hands out. Showing him I mean him no harm. "You're sick right now. Okay? But I'm going to help you. You have to trust me, buddy."

Cheriese was still blubbering behind me. Hal looked at me and immediately I knew the Hal I had known for thirty-odd years was not standing in front of me. Hal was scared and defeated, but even worse, he was already dead.

"It's too late. The stars are falling. It's here." Hal took a step forward and I tried to reach out to him. He kept walking and I took him by his shoulders to hold him back, but he was too slick. He shimmied his way around me, walked up to the nearest stove and turned the burners on.

"My god Hal, *STOP!*" I cried out. But it was too late.

Hal took his hand which was dressed in cooking oil and stuck it over the stove, engulfing his hands in flames. He puts his burning hand up to his face, legs, and everywhere else on his body. Cheriese screamed and tried running after her burning husband until I grabbed her and held her tightly against me.

Don't look. Elizabeth said in my head.

In an instant, I turned Cheriese around and held her head against my chest. Shielding her away from seeing her husband on fire. But I watched. I saw his skin become charred as he stood there. His mouth kept moving until it was only his lips that were too thin to see move. I couldn't hear what he was saying due to Cheriese bawling in my arms. Except I did hear him. In my head.

The Stars are falling. The stars are falling.

Then like a building collapsing he fell to his knees, and finally fell backwards as smoke rose off his corpse. The sprinklers on the ceiling finally came on as if in some sick joke. Putting out the flames as steam came from off Hal's dead body, making the room fill up with a nasty odor (*you've smelt that odor before*) that made it hard to breathe.

"Some… Someone call a goddamn ambulance!" I screamed. Hoping the spectators outside had heard me.

A few minutes later the ambulance arrived. Cheriese had gone into a state of shock. The spectators were all trying to comfort her. Mr. Dickery was being transported into the ambulance. I didn't want to stick around to see them bring Hal out on a gurney. I was so confused and hurt. There was a sound of thunder close by. I looked up at the sky and saw soft gray clouds zooming by. There was something in the sky as well. An orange streak of light or smoke, to this day I still don't know what it was, was streaming in a thin line behind the gray clouds. I looked back down at the mayhem going on in front of me and saw it again.

Don't look at it.

It was the black cat sitting in the middle of the road a block down from the restaurant. I was so mad at what just transpired with Hal that I felt like punting that cat across the road. Ever since I keep running into this bizarre cat, everything has been going to shit.

I pressed my lips together, remembering I needed to check on Linda. I glanced up at the sky once more and that orange streak was still in the sky. The wails of the people, sirens, and Cheriese crying her eyes out all started to fade away. I felt as light as a feather, thinking that the wind could just whisk me away. When I looked back down the road the cat was gone. I started believing that this cat was some sort of hallucination. Oh, how I wish that was true.

It's here.

***

Small droplets of rain started to trickle onto the windshield of my car. I was still processing what took place at Hal's restaurant. And I prayed that everything would be alright with Linda. When I got out of my car after pulling into Linda's driveway the wind just about blew me over. It has been exceedingly picked up since I left the restaurant. Linda lived by herself except for her tiny Yorkie dog. And that little guy was barking up a storm from the backyard.

I knocked on the door and waited. No response. I saw she had one of the doorbells with the little camera in it. I pressed it, waited, and started to speak to the doorbell. "Linda, it's

Kane. You in there?" I paused. "Listen I'm coming in okay?" When I went for the doorknob I found that it was open.

When I went in, the house looked like a tornado had passed through. There were papers, books, spoons, knives, forks, pans, and dog food lying all around. The tv which was mounted off the wall seemed to have been yanked off the wall as the wall mount was barely hanging on the with the tv faced down on the floor. I shouted her name only to have it echo in the empty house. Her tiny yorkie came through the kitchen doggy door from the backyard. I've met him plenty of times, couldn't remember the fuckers name to save my life, but he came up to me, little pudge of a tail wagging. He was shivering but I don't think it was from being cold. I had the feeling he was scared.

I went outside to the backyard to inspect it since that's where I heard the little dog yapping its brains out. There was no sign of her anywhere and now I was starting to get nervous. What if something bad happened to her? And just as worse, what if she's done something bad to someone else? As I was making my way back to the kitchen I noticed a small security camera on top of the door. That gave me an idea.

I returned inside and walked back towards her living room. I searched all around the house until I got to her bedroom. On her dresser was a laptop sitting open. I touched the mouse pad and the screen was exactly what I was looking for. Great minds think alike, even when you're close to peak insanity.

The screen was showing video footage of the front and back porch. Also, there was one in the living room, kitchen, and her room. I clicked around until I saw a playback button. Thinking back on when she should have arrived after the first encounter with the slab, she should have returned home around 6:30. I rewind the footage until I got to yesterday at 6 in the evening and started to play it.

Don't look at the ***...

The recording showed Linda pulling into the driveway and then walking slowly up to the front door. She paused and stood there for a few seconds. Perhaps 30 seconds. Then she walked in and went straight into her bedroom. She opened her laptop exactly where it is right now and did a few click clicks here and there then stepped away from the dresser and just stood there. I waited for a good minute until finally decided to fast-forward it a few minutes ahead. She was still standing there. I did it for an hour. Still standing right where I was standing watching the recording.

Two hours into the recording I stopped it where it was her screaming at the top of her lungs. Her tiny dog was circling her yapping its brains out. Linda picked up her dog and walked with it to the kitchen, opened the door to the back, sat him on the back porch, and closed the door behind her. For a good hour, she was on a rampage of tearing her whole house upside down as if she lost (her mind of course) something of great value to her. Linda did this for at least a good hour before going into her kitchen and started to stare out the door window. She stayed there as still as a mannequin for another good hour, bobbing back and forth as I fast-forward the recording.

Linda finally came around, she opened her back door and stepped out into the backyard. She stopped on the porch and tilted her head sideways examining something (*don't look*) sitting on top of her wooden fence. When she stepped off the porch I saw it was a black cat sitting there staring at Linda with its bright yellow eyes. Her dog yapped at the cat, jumping on the fence trying to climb its way up to attack it. But the cat seemed to not care about the small yapping dog. It just kept staring directly at Linda. She walks up to the cat. Static starts to show on the laptop screen resolving the recording to go in and out.

In a quick instant, a flash of bright orange light shined down from the sky on top of Linda. One minute she was staring up at the sky as the black cat kept staring at her. The next minute she was gone. The cat licked its paw and rubbed its face then hopped off the fence and disappeared.

I shook my head in disbelief at what I just watched. I ran my fingers through my hair due to stress and being scared. Where did she go? And what was that light? Did something come from that orange light?

I pondered.

I went back to the laptop and hit the rewind button to where the orange light was on top of Linda and watched it over again. Seeing her there and then not there. I rewound it and this time slowed the playback. There. Not there. Repeat, slower this time.

There… and then I saw it. In a few short frames, I saw some sort of small creature that looked almost like a squid with a plethora of tentacles. It wrapped its body around Linda then ascended towards the sky and was gone.

I backed away from the laptop. My mind whirled with questions that I knew would never get answers for. I left her room and could hear The little dog yapping again in the backyard. I walked to the kitchen, looked out the window, and could feel my heart racing fiercely. Sitting on top of the fence above the yapping dog was that black cat. My arms were covered in goosebumps. This was no beautiful cat as Elizabeth would have put it, but something purely evil. It was watching me as I stood there behind the door. It sat up, arched its back, and squinched its face giving me a hissing sound with its fur sticking out. Finally, it jumped off the fence to the other side.

I went back into Linda's room to take her laptop with me. Just so I can have the recording to show the world of it later. Too bad I never got to post it.

***

Before I headed back home I went back to the Eastons to check on them again. I pulled up to discover the front door was wide open. I got out and instinctively I looked up at the sky. The clouds were dark gray now with lightning flashing up above. I walked up to the front porch, poking my head in and calling out for Sonny and Vivian. I walked in stepping on broken glass as china vases, glass plates, and other items were thrown around here as well. Seeing so much destruction in the course of a few hours made me feel like the apocalypse had just happened and I was the last of few remaining who survived, now trying to look for scarps and supplies.

I walked around the corner which led to their living room to find Vivian lying dead on the floor in a pool of her blood with six steak knives protruding out of her body. At that point, I couldn't take it anymore. I ran back outside and puked all over the front lawn.

When I was finished I got back into my car. As I started it up I started to feel lightheaded again. My mind was on cloud nine. Images flashed in my head quickly. Finally, the images slowed down and I could see streets and houses burning. Bodies lying all over the ground with intestines out. Stars in the galaxy are going supernova one by one. The earth is now a burning wasteland. Orange space crafts flying all around the sky. The black cat with its piercing yellow eyes. The cat opened its mouth and out came tiny black bugs. A flash of Elizabeth floating in space standing straight up with her back against me. The black cat once again now has tiny black bugs coming out of its eyes and nose. Elizabeth once more now starting to turn around. The black cat now with eyes that resembled the slab the night I brought it home and lit the candle next to it as it was pitch black with tiny white specks. Elizabeth now turned around fully as she was holding the slab in her hands with her eyes completely black with white specks in them.

"It's here," Elizabeth said as it echoed all around me growing louder and louder. "It's here, the stars are falling. Don't look at the cat." She lets out a blood-curdling scream snapping me out of my trance. My hands were gripped tightly to my steering wheel. As I let go I could see a white line now turning red from where I was holding on.

I dawned on something. A quick thought that made me peel out of the Easton driveway and head back to my house. Hoping what I was thinking would be wrong. Yet I knew, with all of the events that just took place I knew I was right as lightning flashes down onto the earth, now raining harder than it ever has before.

***

"If you come across this slab do not touch them," George Stephanopoulos from Good Morning America previously said. "Reports have been coming in from small rural areas across the country of mentally unstable people either killing others along with animals and pets, killing themselves, or even disappearing."

Hal's dead.

Vivian's dead.

Linda's missing.

I'm still alive, but Sonny is also missing. When I pulled into my driveway I could see my front door had been torn down, laying inside of my house. I always kept a small 1.87 Smith and Wesson in the glove compartment of my car. It was fully loaded and only used at the gun range. Hershel was my hometown. I knew everybody and their mamas. Elizabeth never liked the idea of keeping a gun but she did feel safe whenever we would take trips to areas we've never been to. I even took her to the gun range and she was as natural as her beauty.

The wind howled and the rain was rough. Lightning bolts touched down close by as thunder quaked like bombs. I got out of the car, gun in hand. walked up the porch, went into my home, and could hear groaning coming from my den. I cocked the gun and moved slowly towards the groaning noise to find Sonny, shirtless holding a large knife in his hand standing over the slab just staring at it. He was huffing and puffing like the wolf from the Three Pigs story. I could see blood dripping down the tip of the knife as both his hands were full of maroon.

"Sony?" I softly said.

His head slowly pokes up. He turns with a smile from ear to ear. His chest down to his pants was full of blood. His nose seemed broken as it was twisted to the side. Maybe Vivian got one good one in before she lost the battle herself.

"Sonny, let's put down the knife."

"Oh-ho-ho-ho" Sonny chuckled. "Says the man with a gun in his hand."

"What are you doing in my home?"

"I needed to see it, Kane." Sonny took a step forward as I took one back. "I needed to see it. I *needed* to hear it again. They spoke to me Kane, they're here. It's here."

"They?" I raised my gun as he took a step forward and paused. "Who are they? And what in the fuck is here?"

Sonny let out a bottom of the gut laughter that was followed by vicious coughs. "They… are the great old ones. The ones that shaped our world to what it is today. It's here. They told me it was here. My dreams showed me it last night. That there (*dat derr*) tablet told me it's here… the meaning of life."

I shivered at that last part. Sonny has gone mad, and it will only be the same for me in due time. Sonny raised the knife to his head reminding me of a fat Michael Myers. I raised my gun at him, trying to hold it steady as it trembled in my hand. I didn't want to kill Sonny, but if he had left me no choice I would have blown his brains out.

Sonny threw the knife at me like a dart. The tip of the knife grazed my arm as I tried to dodge it while shielding my head. I looked at my arm as a cut on the side of my forearm started gushing with blood. In a quick flash, Sonny came charging at me like a bull. He hit me with his shoulder as I went down and the gun went off shooting the ceiling above us. The gun went spiraling out of my hand. Sonny picked up his knife. I tried getting up but Sonny kicked me in the ribs, damn near rupturing my spleen.

"Sonny," I coughed. "You don't have to do this." I tried crawling to the kitchen table while he was walking towards me.

"Sorry Kane, they told me if I killed you I would be one of the lucky ones to survive. The great old ones have plans for everyone who complies with them. Don't fight this," Sonny began to drool like a rabid dog, " Let me kill you and I'll take that tablet off your hands. It called me first. It should be *MINE!*"

The tablet is yours. Elizabeth's voice said in my head. Sonny kicked me once more this time in the head. I lay flat on my stomach and at that moment I started to see a bright light as if I was just about to die. I wasn't sure if it was from the kick or just me starting to lose my mind as well, but on the other end of the table, there she stood. Elizabeth. Standing with a bright aura around her. Like an angel right out of heaven. *You don't have to fight him. It'll all be over soon anyway. Just don't look at the cat.*

At that moment I could feel something in my hands. It was the slab. I could feel the vibrations as it was pulsing stronger than ever before. I looked deep into it and could see tiny white specks beginning to float off of the slab, rising high into the air.

The stars are falling. Lightning flashed into my house as thunder made the entire place shake.

"I'm sorry again, Kane," Sonny said, standing over me. "But I gots to kill ya now." He flips me over by my shoulder with a laugh. As I turned over I used the slab to crack it over Sonny's head. He takes a tumble backward. Shot up to my feet, searching all over for my gun. Sonny was regaining himself as he shook his head. Blood sprayed everywhere from his broken nose.

"You Goddamn son of a bitch!" Sonny roared. "I'm gonna kill ya! I'm gonna-." He paused then dropped his knife. "It's you. You were in my dreams. Did I do good?"

Confused as he was talking to someone behind me. And it wasn't someone but *something*. I turned and saw it was the black cat sitting between the den and the kitchen. I could feel the air growing thin. The sound of rain crashing from the sky sounded like little pebbles.

"I was going to kill him, I swear." Sonny blubbered as he wiped the blood from his nostrils.

Silence.

"What… What do you mean?"

Silence. Thunder quaking outside.

"No. No, no, no, no, *NO!* I did everything you said I needed to do. You told me it's here and I -."

"*Meow.*" The black cat said in the lowest tone I have ever heard a cat give. The cat then started to arch its back and started hacking, its stomach going in and out as if it was about to puke up a hairball. Instead, black tar-like matter started spewing from the cat's mouth. Smoke started rising off the black vomit. The cat's back started cracking as its spine started to grow bigger. It leaped onto its hind legs and started to morph into something I couldn't even explain.

Don't look at the cat! Elizabeth wailed into my head. I turned to face Sonny with my back against the cat. I felt scared not knowing what was happening behind me as the cat made a groaning sound like a human would. Only it didn't sound human. It sounded like nothing in this world I had ever heard. More bones cracked behind me. A shadow was forming, growing larger by the second. I could see a huge creature with four arms that seemed to be tentacles of some sort. I watched as Sonny's mouth was agape, shivering like the yapping dog back at Linda's. His eyes grew wild as blood started to flow down them. Sonny begins to whimper and then begins to scream at the creature behind me.

Don't look. Don't look. Don't look.

Sonny then started to make a run towards my torn-down front door when the creature behind me bellowed out. It charged right past me and as it did my head went straight down as did my heart as it was ready to leap out of my asshole. I could hear Sonny pleading to the monster as I heard it catch up to him.

Curiosity killed the cat.

I couldn't help myself. But now thinking about it I think it was the slab that told me (*look up, see what you're missing*) to get a glimpse of this creature. I looked up at the creature chasing Sonny. It used its tentacle arm to swipe at Sonny's feet. He fell hard. Sonny turned to his back and tried crawling away. The creature took all four tentacles and pierced them into Sonny's body and head. The creature's back was all spine as it poked out showing the many grooves in its back. It was still black but it was no longer a cat. Its head was round and earless. The legs were jagged and hairy. I'm sure if I had seen its face I would have not been able to tell you my story.

Sonny had broken down into a seizure as he screamed at the creature draining away my once neighbor. He withered down until he was just skin and bones as his screams started to fade.

The creature bellowed out again before taking its tentacles out of Sonny. *Don't look.* I looked back down at my feet. I heard the creature give a gruff as I felt its eyes staring down at me. It slowly walked towards me. Now it was me shivering like Linda's yapping dog. The creature stood above me as I saw its feet which reminded me of hooves. Its breath was vile and I remembered that this smell was from the slab. I looked at my hand and saw the slab glowing with a multitude of colors all at once. That kept me in a trance for god knows how long. I closed my eyes. When I opened them I was in space floating in front of Elizabeth.

"You did good my love," Elizabeth said to me as it echoed all around us. "We are the stars that must fall. Prophecies from the old ones spoke to me before I passed on. They told me that it is here, the route of life. The route of death. The route... to an everlasting paradise. We must first be able to handle it. Don't look at the cat or you will go into madness. The cat has been here since before the dawn of man. To the universe, it has many names. But the one we gave it here is Death. The hearts that have been tormented in the dark will finally have their time to come and their time to rest. It's almost your time. Do not be afraid. It's only a matter of a little pain."

I opened my eyes and the hooves of the cat were gone. I slowly looked up to see I was alone and that the cat was gone. The slab in my hand was now once more its original metallic color as the vibrations went back down to a slow hum.

Only a matter of a little pain.

I wanted to throw the slab hard against the wall, and yet something advised me that would be a bad idea. And to this day as I write, the slab is still in my possession. To this day I believe I'll die with this slab.

***

The sky is now a bleak gray. Orange smoke streaks race across the sky as nighttime falls. I sit at the very top of my roof to get a good look at the show. In a few minutes, it'll finally be time. My time. Our time. Everyone's time. The ones with torment in their hearts. As darkness falls I can hear screams all around me. Was it coming from town? Other towns? States? Countries?

It's only a matter of pain, right? One star falls far off in the distance making a huge explosion. Then one by one they all start coming down.

My god.

The stars are falling. The stars are falling. The stars are falling. The stars are falling. The stars are falling. The stars are falling. The stars....

www.ingramcontent.com/pod-product-compliance
Lightning Source LLC
Chambersburg PA
CBHW070016260626
47159CB00005B/1830